Me

Nicholas Mosley, born in 1923, is the author of a dozen novels, most recently the Whitbread Award-winning *Hopeful Monsters*. Films have been made of two of his novels, *Accident* (using a screenplay by Harold Pinter and directed by Joseph Losey) and *Impossible Object*. He has also written non-fiction books on politics and religion, and an autobiography, *Efforts at Truth*. He is currently working on a new novel. He has five children and lives with his second wife in London.

Also by Nicholas Mosley

Spaces of the Dark
The Rainbearers
Corruption
Accident*
Assassins*
Impossible Object*
Natalie Natalia*
Catastrophe Practice*
Imago Bird*
Judith*
Serpent*
Hopeful Monsters*
African Switchback
The Life of Raymond Raynes
Experience and Religion
The Assassination of Trotsky
Julian Grenfell
Rules of the Game
Beyond the Pale
Efforts at Truth

available in Minerva

NICHOLAS MOSLEY

Meeting Place

Minerva

A Minerva Paperback
MEETING PLACE

First published in Great Britain 1962
by Weidenfeld & Nicolson
This revised Minerva edition published 1995
by Mandarin Paperbacks
an imprint of Reed Books Ltd
Michelin House, 81 Fulham Road, London SW3 6RB
and Auckland, Melbourne, Singapore and Toronto

A CIP catalogue record for this title
is available from the British Library
ISBN 0 7493 9601 6

Phototypeset by Intype, London
Printed and bound in Great Britain
by Cox & Wyman Ltd, Reading, Berkshire

I

The telephone rang. Harry picked it up and held the mouthpiece under his chin. He watched the lighted windows of a huge office building opposite. He said 'Connaught 2468, can I help you?'

The façade of the office building took up most of the view. On one side was a vertical strip of dark sky. The windows seemed to light up a frieze of two dimensions – a man with a desk and a pile of papers on it, repeatedly.

Harry said 'Where are you speaking from?'

Harry was in a smaller building. The frame of its window was of stone and went up into a point. There was a table with a typewriter in front of him. No sound came from the telephone.

'It's been cold today,' Harry said. 'Have you got a fire?'

A voice on the telephone said 'No.'

Harry raised the mouthpiece. 'Can you come round here?'

'Are you the people . . .?' the voice said.

'Yes.'

'What do you do?'

'Are you in London?'

'Highgate,' the voice said.

'Then change at King's Cross, you know where we are?'

There was silence again. Harry said 'We can talk.' In one of the windows opposite a man swivelled in his chair and stretched his feet out. Harry lowered his head so that it almost touched his knees. He said 'What's been happening today, what's the trouble?'

The door of the room in which he was sitting opened and a woman came in. She wore a blue coat and had neat wavy hair. She carried a shopping bag. She paid no attention to Harry. She went to the gas fire and took off her coat.

The voice on the telephone said 'Are you there?'

'Yes,' Harry said.

'What do you say to people?'

'Come round.'

'I can't.'

'Have you had anything to eat today?'

'Why?' the voice said.

'You could have a cup of tea and some food.'

'I hadn't got any matches,' the voice said. There was a coughing sound, then silence.

Harry lifted his head and stretched his eyes affectedly. The woman knelt by the fire and opened and shut her fingers. 'Do you live alone?' Harry said.

'Yes.'

'Couldn't you get some matches?' The woman took some tins and packages out of the paper bag. 'Have you been out today?'

'No.'

'And you wanted some food.'

2

'Yes.'

Harry looked out of the window again. There was a girl leaning on the desk beside the man with his feet out. She had the toe of one foot behind the other, pointing towards the ground. 'Did you turn the gas on?' Harry said.

'Yes,' the voice said.

'Then turn it off.'

'Why?'

'I'll come round,' Harry said.

He reached for a pad of paper on the table in front of him. The woman by the fire stood up, took a pencil, and gave it to him. He began writing *I've got to go* then stopped, tearing off the top sheet of paper. He said into the telephone 'Good, now what's your name?' He wrote *Bill* on the second sheet of paper. 'And your address?' He went on writing.

The woman leaned on the table. Harry stretched out a hand and lifted the sleeve of her coat. She turned her wrist towards him so that he could see her watch. He made a face and pointed at the telephone. 'I'll be with you,' he said. He half stood up, putting the second sheet of paper into his pocket. He pulled the first sheet towards him and wrote *this awful committee*. The woman looked at it. He said 'All right, fine.' He moved round the table still listening on the telephone. 'See you,' he said. He put the receiver down.

He went to the door. The woman sat down in the chair that he had left. 'I'm late,' he said. He picked up a briefcase. 'Thanks, Helen.'

'Was that person all right?' Helen said.

3

'Oh he was all right,' Harry said. He went out.

From the middle of the back wall of a committee room a crucifix hung with its top pointing slightly outwards. On either side were portraits of white-haired clergymen in ermine. A table stretched down the middle around which several clergymen were seated, with some laymen in tweed suits and one nun. In a high-backed chair beneath the crucifix was a priest of about forty in the habit of a monk. He had a thin bony face and close-cropped hair. He said 'Gentlemen – '

The people round the table faced inwards and picked up papers. Someone said 'And lady – '

'I think we'd better get on,' the monk said.

'And lady,' several people repeated. They laughed and pointed towards the nun.

'Oh I'm sorry,' the monk said. He stared at the nun.

'Mr Gates told me he might be late,' the monk went on. 'You've had the minutes, so can I take them as read? The matters arising are on the agenda, so we can take them from there. First there's the report of the Help Thy Neighbour Service. Can I have your opinions?'

People picked up their papers and shuffled them and looked at the ones in the hands of the people beside them. A man in a tweed suit said 'I never got one of these.'

A clergyman in a black jacket said 'Couldn't we have a rule that notices go out to give a fortnight's notice?'

'Can I take it that the report and recommendations are accepted?' the monk said.

'Oh just a minute,' a Scotch voice said. A tall man

with white hair stood up. 'Do I understand we've already passed the minutes?'

'Yes,' the monk said.

'I'm not completely up with the rest of the field.' The Scotchman moved his papers about. 'Like Alice, I don't know where to begin. But as a Scotchman I'd like to ask first – where does the money go?'

'Page four,' the monk said.

'What these accounts show,' the Scotchman said, 'is the truth of Mr Micawber's famous dictum – income one pound, expenditure nineteen and sixpence, result happiness. Income one pound, expenditure one pound and sixpence, result misery.'

'Income twenty pounds,' the nun said.

The Scotchman stared at his papers.

'Mr Micawber,' the nun said.

'Twenty pounds,' the Scotchman said. 'Oh.' He put one or two papers from the back of his pile to the front. 'But perhaps Sister Hilary won't dispute my exegesis.' He smiled and bowed down the table. 'I'm enough of a Marxist to want to know not only how the money goes, but what are its results. I think we should know this before we are *asked for more.*' He spoke these last words as if they were a quotation.

A man wearing an old Etonian tie said 'I'm rather horrified by our investments.'

A bald priest in a black cassock said 'We should ship into industrials.'

The door opened and Harry Gates came in. He carried his briefcase and wore an overcoat. He said 'I'm so sorry.' He moved to a vacant chair while taking off his coat, one sleeve of which got stuck over the briefcase. He sat down with the coat inside out and the briefcase under it on his knees. The monk watched him.

'Perhaps you'd like to ask Mr Gates some questions,' the monk said.

The Scotchman said 'I'd be grateful.' He put a thumb in his waistcoat pocket, took it out, smoothed a coat lapel and said 'My anxiety is no doubt due more to deficiencies of accounting than of organization.' His thumb moved up to the rim of his ear. He went on talking.

Harry had disentangled his hand from his coat and he rummaged through the pile of papers in front of him. He found one with a blank space at the bottom, tore it off, and began writing on it. He held his other arm bent round to keep it hidden. When he had finished he folded the paper into a strip and wrote FR. PATTERSON on it in capital letters. He passed it to his neighbour, pointing to the monk in the chair beneath the crucifix.

'. . . a more detailed breakdown,' the Scotchman said. He sat down.

'Mr Gates?' the monk said.

Harry stood up, sent his chair tipping backwards, caught it, began 'Yes of course. . . .' His neighbour had passed the piece of paper round the table till it had reached the man in the old Etonian tie, who began to open it. '. . . I'll do my best,' Harry said. A man whispered 'Father Patterson.' 'What?' the man in the old Etonian tie said. 'I mean, what we want is two hundred pounds,' Harry said. He picked up his papers. 'I don't do the accounts, actually, but that's what it looks like.

6

The expenses are rates, heating, lighting, fares, travel, that sort of thing.' 'Oh sorry,' the man in the old Etonian tie said: the piece of paper moved on again. Harry said 'There are twelve of us in the office, and we take it in turns. Father Wodehouse is in charge, but he's ill at the moment. Others help with the outside work of course. We get all sorts of calls, a lot at night. We help people in trouble, mostly at some dead end. Suicides.' He ran his hand through his hair. 'We get them to come to us or go to them. It's partly just someone to talk to, and partly practical. We help with jobs or money.' He broke off, staring at the table.

The piece of paper had reached the monk, who began to unfold it. When he had got half-way he saw written on it *I've got to go* and underneath *dinne* and at the bottom *Palomede*. The ends of each line were cut off by a fold. The monk doubled up the paper again and put it in his pocket.

'I mean if you can give us some money, please do,' Harry said. 'We'd be grateful.' He scratched his head again. 'We only claim expenses. But if you can't, don't – I expect we'll get it somehow.' The Scotchman stared at his knees. 'As a matter of fact someone rang us up just as I was coming here,' Harry said, 'he actually had the gas on, or said he did. I said I'd go round. I think I better.' He began picking up his coat, which was inside out. 'I'm so sorry.' He got one arm in the sleeve and pulled it and it came out limply. 'We were very grateful for the money last time. If there's anything else – ' He moved towards the door.

'Did he turn it off?' the monk said.

'What?' Harry said. 'Oh yes.' He seemed momentarily convulsed with giggles. Then he went out.

'Shall we vote on the recommendations?' the monk said.

The restaurant Chez Palomede has an outer and inner door so that people who come in pass through a glass compartment like a telephone box. Jenny saw a man with a briefcase come in and peer through the glass and then wait in the compartment reading a newspaper.

Jenny was at a table for two with a man in a grey suit and dark blue shirt. He had black curly hair and yellow eyes that seemed to have no pupils to them. His arm was along the back of the sofa-seat behind Jenny. He was saying 'The difference between being in love and loving is the same as between a child and an adult: in the one you project yourself, and in the other you recognize a separate person.' His hand strayed from the back of the seat and touched Jenny on her neck. 'Perhaps you don't know the difference.'

'Thanks,' Jenny said. She reached for her handbag, opened it, took out a pair of spectacles of which one of the side-pieces was missing, and held them on her nose like lorgnettes.

'Love is the recognition of another person's freedom,' the man said. His hand moved up Jenny's neck. 'It involves a certain suffering.' He reached the lobe of her ear, and moved over it. 'Are you listening?'

'I can't,' Jenny said.

The man in the glass partition had been joined by a monk in a black cassock. They were laughing. They came through the inner door and spoke to the head waiter. The first man was tall with a rather bony face and dark eyes. The waiter led them up the restaurant. Jenny and the man with curly hair watched them.

'But we got the money?' Harry was saying.

'Oh goodness yes,' Father Patterson said.

'Well that's what matters.'

They went to the far end of the room. The restaurant was crowded. Jenny saw them standing while the head waiter peered round tables. The man with black curly hair said 'When I see a priest I want to cross myself.'

'Why?' Jenny said.

'I think their compensations are obscene.'

Harry and Father Patterson were coming back down the restaurant. The waiter stopped at the table where Jenny and the man were sitting. He pulled back two empty chairs opposite the sofa seat. He said 'If you would not mind, it will not be two minutes.' 'I'm so sorry,' Harry said. He noticed the man with black curly hair and said 'Hullo, Jerril.' The man smiled briefly. Harry and Father Patterson sat down.

Harry said to Father Patterson 'He was in a bed-sitter, you know – a room with nothing in it but a gas fire and enough blankets to put along the bottom of the door – a hopeless man, twenty-six, wife left him, job gone, drink, debts, diabetes – ' at each word Harry gesticulated and stretched his eyes; Father Patterson began to laugh; ' – he was knocked down in the street by a milk-float, one of those things that go along like a pram – ' Father Patterson's laughter boomed through the restaurant: ' – and this made him lose his sense of balance, which

9

was disastrous, as he's a steeplejack.' Harry suddenly noticed the girl opposite him. She had amber-coloured hair and wore pale lipstick and had black lines around her eyes.

'Oh how wonderful!' Father Patterson said.

Harry lowered his hand in the middle of a gesture.

Jenny looked away. The man with the curly hair had closed his eyes and folded his hands in his lap. Father Patterson had taken out a handkerchief and was making a pad of it to blow his nose. Harry stared at the wall above Jenny's head.

'Your table is ready,' the waiter said.

Harry and Father Patterson stood up. Harry bowed to Jenny. He said 'Thank you.'

When they had gone the man with curly hair shivered and said 'I feel contaminated.' Jenny said 'Didn't he know you?' 'It's like lifting a rock,' the man said, 'and seeing the middle ages coming out.' 'But who is he?' Jenny said.

'His name's Harry Gates.'

'What's wrong with him?'

Jenny leaned forward and put her one-sided spectacles on her nose. Harry and Father Patterson were sitting at their table.

'He was particularly dreadful to his wife,' the man called Jerril said.

In the middle of the night Harry sat alone in the office where the window was of stone and went up to a point. There was no light in the façade of the huge office building opposite. A sound of snoring came from the next room. Harry was writing:

Dear Father Wodehouse,
The League of Charity gave us £200. Father Patterson was very good. I hope we can expand a bit soon. I wonder if we could think of a better name.

He tipped his chair back. He stared at the ceiling and screwed up his face in a theatrical gesture. He said 'I do hate the night!' He put his feet on the table and folded his hands in his lap. After a time he sat forward again and tore the top sheet off a writing pad and wrote –

Amber of your honey hair
Ambergris of gold and bone
Tangled honey lend the bees
Your honeycomb

He crossed out 'bone' in the second line and wrote 'stone' above it: then crossed out this, searched for a rubber, and put back 'bone'.

The telephone rang. He picked up the receiver and said 'Connaught 2468, can I help you?'

'Oh *do*' a drawling voice said.

Harry narrowed his mouth with his lips turned inwards. He put the receiver under his chin.

'Don't you want to know what I *want*?' the voice said.

'Yes,' Harry said.

'*You*, the voice said. There were suppressed giggles in the distance.

'Can you come round here?' Harry said.

There was a short silence. Then – 'Wouldn't it be nicer if you came here?' It was a man's voice, putting on an effeminate accent.

'No,' Harry said.

There was another silence. Harry was taking deep breaths through his nose. The man's voice changed. 'This is a *joke*.'

'I know,' Harry said.

He heard the person breathing at the other end. His own heart was thumping. He said 'Come round, any time, you know where we are.'

The voice suddenly said in a natural accent 'Good night.'

'Good night,' Harry said. There was the dialling tone.

He put the receiver down and looked round the room. There was a filing cabinet, a bookcase, a door to the passage, four chairs in a row, the gas fire and ring with a kettle on it, a teapot and three mugs on the floor, a map of North London on the wall, the door into an inner room where the snoring was coming from, his table with the telephone and typewriter. He saw the piece of paper with the poem written on it and he crumpled it.

He went to the window and put his forehead against the glass. He said 'Oh God, help us.'

The telephone rang. He went back to the table and said 'Connaught 2468, can I help you?'

There was no reply. He waited, as usual, with the

mouthpiece under his chin. He said 'Where are you speaking from?'

A voice said 'Is that you?'

He went cold from his throat to his fingers. He seemed to be watching himself from slightly above – the set of his face that he could not stop being theatrical. He said 'Annie?'

There was silence again, and after a time a click and then the dialling tone.

The woman stood in the dark with her hand on the receiver. She was in a room with no curtains and a bare wooden floor. There was the smell of dust. The lights of a car went past in the street below and swept the room in elongating patterns. They lit a jumble of packing-cases and old furniture and one armless statue at an angle against the wall. The telephone was on a three-legged chair propped by books. The woman listened. There were footsteps beyond the door, and a low voice talking. They seemed to go into another room on the same landing. A door closed.

She waited. She heard slight movements as if furniture were being moved. Another car went past, changing gear. She went to the door of the room and unlocked it. On the landing there was a flight of stairs descending. She went down on tiptoe. On the next landing a door was open and in darkness. She switched on a light, which lit up an L-shaped room with an easel and some stacked paintings in a corner and on the floor a huge frame of plate glass. Two armchairs faced each other. There was a stool between them, and on it a handbag

13

and a pair of spectacles of which one of the sidepieces was missing.

The woman turned off the light. She went to the ground floor. Passing a mirror she looked at herself briefly. Her face was white. She wore a black jersey and skirt and had dark hair. She went out of the front door into the street.

She turned and walked along the railings. A car started up behind and came towards her in low gear. There were shadows across the street from houses which cut off the moon. The car crossed the road so that it was on the wrong side close to her. A man leaned out of the window and peered at her as he drove. He said 'Where are *you* going?' The woman walked on. The car ground along beside her. The man said 'Give you a lift, Miss?' He laughed. The woman paid no attention. 'It's the fortnightly check-up,' he said: 'coming quietly?'

He accelerated and pulled up twenty yards ahead of her and switched off the engine. He got out and leaned against the mudguard and waited. When she was close to him she stopped. 'My pretty maid,' the man said. The woman said 'Oh have you been waiting long, poor Maurice?'

The man took hold of her arm. He had a handsome florid face with hair cut in clear lines like a film star. He wore a brown suede jacket and tartan trousers. He said 'Come along.'

'You were just passing!' the woman said. She walked round the car and climbed in. The man sat in the driving seat. He said, 'Where were you going?'

14

'Waterloo Bridge,' the woman said. She had assumed an affected sing-song voice.

The man started the car and drove to a square with plane trees and a garden. He stopped again. He said 'I want to know the truth.'

'Oh the truth!' the woman said.

'It's important,' the man called Maurice said. He put his arm along the back of her seat. She was staring in front of her. 'It's only by the truth you can trust anyone.' His hand strayed down and touched her neck. 'You must have trust;' his hand reached her ear; 'to respect the other person.'

The woman burst out laughing. She had a deep rather masculine laugh. She said 'You sound like Jerril.'

She laid her head against the back of her seat. The man put his fingers round her throat. A muscle moved in his cheek as if he were chewing. He said 'Hm?'

The woman smiled. His hand pressed against her throat. After a time she sat up and pushed his hand away. She said 'Let's go home, I'm tired.'

Harry Gates rang the bell of a front door within the porch of which green leaves climbed amongst wrought-iron railings and a stained-glass fan-light showed the bright colours of birds. He unfolded a morning paper and read ARCHIE GOES TO WORK and underneath it *Biggest Satellite In Orbit*. A butler opened the front door and said 'Good morning, Mr Gates.'

'Hullo, Parks, is Lady Sykes in?'

'Doctor Johnson's with her.'

'Is she ill?'

15

'No,' the butler said.

Harry went through into a hall where two life-sized statues of negro children stood on either side of a wooden chest on which there was a glass dome containing a stuffed fish. Harry said 'Can I go up?'

'Oh I think so,' the butler said.

Harry went to the second floor and knocked on a door and when there was no answer opened it and put his head into a bedroom. On the wall opposite him was a large frame containing what looked like splintered triplex glass. Round the corner was a bed with a striped canopy above it. There was no one in the room. The bed was littered with papers and opened letters. There was another door on his right, encrusted with dominoes. He called – 'Susannah?'

A voice on the far side of the door said 'Oh it's you.'

Harry sat in the bedroom in a pink armchair stuffed in the shape of a shell. He unfolded his paper and read *Another of man's dreams comes true – the flying laboratory*. There was a picture of a man with a bow-tie and close-cropped hair. From behind the door with dominoes Harry heard voices.

When the door opened a woman came in wearing an elaborate dressing-gown with a collar up the back like a ruff. A towel was round her head and her face shone. She was followed by a small middle-aged man with heavy, hooded eyelids. Harry stood up. The woman said 'May I introduce my brother Harry, Doctor Johnson.' She sat at a dressing-table and wiped her face.

Doctor Johnson said 'How do you do.' He turned away. He stood in the middle of the room and rattled money in his pockets. Harry folded his paper. Doctor Johnson said 'Lydia, can I take the car, you're not using it, are you?' He spoke quietly, almost muttering, in a faint foreign accent.

The woman said 'Don't you want to talk to Harry?'

He came over and stood by Harry, almost touching. He said 'Why did you call Lydia Susannah?'

'She was in the bath,' Harry said.

Doctor Johnson rattled his money. He said 'You were a friend of Annie Longley's, weren't you?'

'Yes,' Harry said.

'I see her once or twice.' He tailed off.

'How is she?'

His hooded eyes lowered. 'Physically?'

'Yes,' Harry said.

'I don't know.'

'Or any other way.'

'She was with Maurice – wasn't she – you know Maurice?'

'Yes,' Harry said.

Doctor Johnson went back and stood by the dressing-table. He said 'Lydia, can I take the car, to go back, you're not using it. . . .'

'Ask Parks' the woman said. She went to her bed and lay down. She closed her eyes.

Doctor Johnson came back and stood by Harry, staring at his coat. He said 'She hasn't come to me professionally.'

'No,' Harry said.

'No,' Doctor Johnson said. He moved to the door. He went out.

Harry sat down again. He read in the newspaper *Archie is so called after Ancient Greek Scientist Archimedes (287–212 B.C.) who said 'Give me a place to stand and I will move the earth.'* Harry said 'How are you?'

'I'm all right,' Lydia said. She opened her eyes. 'Why aren't you helping your neighbours?'

'I am.'

'You must have been pushed to come here.'

'You know I love seeing you,' Harry said.

'You mortify yourself,' Lydia said.

Harry said – 'Annie rang me up last night.'

Lydia sat up and turned her head. 'Did she?'

'At the office, I mean. She rang off when I answered. But I think it was her. I don't know if she knew I was there.'

'Well I don't know,' Lydia said. She watched him. 'She might have rung off anyway.'

'She might,' Harry said.

'Or she must have known. Have you seen her?'

'Not for two or three months.'

'What do you want me to do?'

'Could you find out?' Harry said. He stood up. 'I didn't know where to find her. I want to know if she's all right. I'll go over at lunch-time to that pub where Maurice goes.' He walked over to the picture on the wall that looked like splintered glass. He said 'Is this Jerril?'

'Yes,' Lydia said.

He put out a hand and touched it. 'It *is* glass.'

'Don't you think it's pretty?' Lydia said.

18

Harry went and stood by the end of her bed. She lay with the towel round her head like a turban. Her mouth was in a narrow colourless line. She stared back at him.

'Are you o.k.?' Harry said.

'Yes,' she said.

'Who is this Doctor Johnson?'

'A witch-doctor.'

'What does he do?'

Lydia said – 'How are your awful neighbours?'

'Does he talk about our family?'

Lydia said – 'He's not an analyst.' She sat up and reached for a leather-bound book on the bed. 'Come and have dinner, I'll find out about Annie. Tonight?'

'I'll try,' Harry said.

'Just say you will or you won't.'

'I will,' Harry said.

Helen Mason sat in the room with the window that went up into a point. She was typing with two fingers. Opposite her on a rickety chair sat a man in rumpled clothes and a red face. Helen said 'Mr Gates may be in later.'

'It doesn't matter,' the man said.

'Bill, isn't it? Did he see you last night?'

'Yes, he was very good to me.' The man sat with a hand on each knee and leaned slightly forwards. He frowned, as if trying to catch what Helen was saying.

'Did I see you had a limp?' Helen said.

'I was knocked down by a milk lorry.'

'What rotten luck. Are you under a doctor?'

'I'm better now,' the man said. Whenever Helen

19

looked at him, he smiled. 'There's nothing like Christianity.'

'Are you a Christian?' Helen said.

'Oh yes,' the man said. 'I wasn't once. I was in a terrible state – drinking – oh – I wouldn't like to tell you!'

'Then what happened?' Helen said.

The man stared at her. He was slightly cross-eyed. He began to speak, stopped, then smiled.

Helen went on typing. The telephone rang. Helen said 'Connaught 2468, can I help you?' She listened for a while and then said 'Thank you, I will. . . . I will get. . . .' She turned a pencil round in her fingers. 'No, not me.' She listened again. 'Yes,' she said. She put the receiver down.

She said, 'We're in trouble.'

'I was all over the place,' the man said. 'I was in debt – '

Helen dialled a number and listened. When there was no reply she put the receiver down and dialled again.

'I owe six weeks rent,' the man said. 'My landlord – oh – he isn't a Christian.'

'How much is that?' Helen said.

'Six weeks at two pounds ten, that's. . . .'

'Couldn't you get anywhere cheaper?' Helen said. She put the receiver down.

'Mr Gates was wonderful to me,' the man said.

'Have you got a job?' Helen was looking up a number in the telephone book.

'I start on Monday,' the man said. He breathed

through his mouth. 'A new building site, you could ring them.'

Helen closed the telephone book. She put a hand to her forehead and stroked it down her temple. Her face went peculiarly flat and impersonal.

'I think we're in the world to help one another,' the man said. 'That's the point, isn't it?'

The telephone rang. Helen picked up the receiver and said 'Connaught 2468, can I help you?' and then – 'Oh thank goodness, Harry, can you do something?'

Annie emerged into the sunlight wearing her black jersey and skirt and carrying a coat over her arm. She was in a main street with buses jammed behind one another, shaking. It was a fine day with the clouds moving. She walked up the line of traffic. At a crossroads there were policemen on motor-bikes. They wore polished boots and crash-helmets with chin-straps hanging down. They leaned on one leg and waved the traffic on.

Annie looked in shop windows. There were dummies of girls with dark faces and pale pink eyes and silver lips. They stood with their feet apart and their hips out and their wrists curved like the necks of swans. At another window there was a girl in a bathing dress lying on her back with her knees in the air and a man leaning over her with dark brown skin and a gold moustache.

Annie walked on. A small crowd had collected on the pavement. They were watching a lorry parked in the middle of the road with a raised platform and scaffolding and pulleys. Some men were raising a contraption of coloured bulbs and wires to hang between two lamp-posts. The contraption was the figure of a woman, supported at the neck and feet with ropes and holding what looked like a wand in one hand and a ball in the other. A voice said 'What will they think of?' A man in a blue suit stood beside Annie. 'It's not even Christmas,' Annie said. 'Two hundred and fifty shopping days,' the man said. 'How clever to know!' Annie said. She looked up again in profile, smiling with her teeth. The figure was being hauled upright by the neck. 'Everything's advertising, advertising,' the man said.

Annie moved on. The man followed her. She went down a side street, past a church with an enormous thermometer outside and a red line half-way up. The man caught up with her and said 'What a world, isn't it?' An alarm bell suddenly began ringing somewhere above their heads. The man said 'Would you like some coffee?'

'No thank you,' Annie said.

The man stood on the steps of the church. Annie went into a telephone box. There was a newspaper on the shelf. She dialled a number and a woman's voice answered her and said 'Connaught 2468, can I help you?'

Annie looked at herself in the mirror. Her white face was slightly crumpled like papier mâché. She heard the woman talking to someone else on the end of the wire: the voice said 'What will be your wages?'

Annie turned the newspaper round and read *What is in the satellite?* Lower down on the same page she read *Lord Sykes, Minister of State, returns to London today after visiting the Prime Minister*. She put the receiver down.

When she stepped out into the street the man in the blue suit said 'Please have some coffee, I'd like to talk.' His face looked terrified. Annie screwed her eyes up into the sun. Above her was a neon sign of a goose with a large yellow egg.

'I'm lonely,' the man said.

Annie saw a taxi passing and hailed it. She ran into the road. A car braked sharply. The taxi stopped. Annie said 'Fleet Street, please,' climbing in.

Harry and a thick-set man in an ex-army leather jerkin and gumboots stood in a yard of a row of back-to-back houses. They were between an outside lavatory which seemed collapsing and a scullery window which they faced. Half-way out of this window leaned a large woman in a blue flowered dress. She had an elaborate iron-grey hairstyle. She seemed to be jammed in the window, like the figurehead of a ship.

The man in gumboots said 'If it was me I'd get the police, we pay enough taxes.'

The woman half out of the window said 'I'm not letting him get away with it.'

The man said 'That Miss Mason who was here last time, she said not to ring the police, but to call her. So I rang, but if it was me I'd put young Mick where they'd learn him, but I'm only the lodger.'

'Where is Mick?' Harry said.

'He's in the back room, locked, he's got a knife, he's near had a piece out of her already.'

23

'He's not getting away with it this time,' the woman in the window said.

'Can he get into the scullery?' Harry said.

'He better not,' the man in gumboots said.

'You stay here,' Harry said. 'Mrs Jackson, don't move.'

'She can't!' the man in gumboots said. He brayed with laughter.

Harry went in at the back door. There was a passage with some stairs on his right. On the left were two doors. He opened the far one and looked into a sitting-room which was empty. The near door was closed. He stood by it. He heard faint tinny music inside. He said 'Mick!' Then – 'My name's Harry Gates, I'm a friend of Helen Mason's, she couldn't come round but she asked me to.'

The music stopped. The door had four panels inset and was stained dark. The handle was of crumpled brass. Harry squatted and looked into the keyhole. There was a key on the other side.

'I'd like to come in,' Harry said. 'No one'll come with me.'

There was silence; then a violent banging some distance away. The woman in the scullery began shouting. Harry went out at the back and met the man in gumboots coming in. The man in gumboots said 'Break the door!' Harry turned the man round and went out with him into the yard. The woman still projected from the window. She was chewing her lip steadily. 'He hasn't got in?' Harry said.

'If he does he'll do her,' the man said.

'He doesn't want to get in!' Harry shouted.

24

He went back into the passage and stood by the door with the crumpled handle. The banging had stopped. He said 'They haven't sent for the police yet, Mick, but they will.' He crossed his legs and rested his head against the door. His face had gone peculiarly flat and tired. 'And what's the good of that?' The brass handle moved slightly, and there was a scraping noise. Harry waited. He said 'Thanks, Mick.' He opened the door.

The room was a kitchen-parlour with a black polished iron range and new brown furniture with mirrors inlaid and two modern adjustable armchairs. A television set was switched on and on the screen a man was holding up a spherical object and pointing at it, but no sound came from his mouth. By a far door stood a boy of about fifteen wearing tight black trousers and a white shirt and striped tie. He had a squarish face with greased hair sticking up along the top. He did not look at Harry.

Harry said 'I'm Harry Gates.' He looked at the television. He said 'Is that the satellite?'

The boy looked up. The man on the screen was turning the spherical object round in his fingers. The scene changed to a diagram of a black circle with a silver line going round it. 'I wonder what's in it,' Harry said. He sat on the arm of a chair. The silver line stopped, and dotted lines went off it in several directions. 'You better come with me, Mick, till all this quietens.'

'What quietens?' the boy said.

'Your mother thinks you've gone at her with a knife, and she'll call the police if you're still here.'

'I don't – ' the boy said.

'She's afraid and angry.'

25

'What's she got – ' the boy said. His words got cut off each time like a sneeze.

'But that's what she thinks,' Harry repeated. He was still watching the television. The boy was holding something in his hand and rubbing his knuckles with it.

'She won't let me alone,' the boy said.

'It'd be better if you got away for a while, I'll talk to her,' Harry stood up. 'I've got the car.'

The boy's face was pink and swollen. He started across the room towards Harry. Harry was turning the television off when he heard voices outside. He looked out of the back window and saw the man in gumboots by the scullery and another figure beyond him. They were talking to the woman in the scullery window. The third figure moved towards the back door and Harry saw it was a policeman. 'Blast,' Harry said. He stood by the door of the room. 'Have you got a knife, Mick, give it to me.' The boy looked out of the window. Harry held the handle of the door behind him and he heard footsteps coming along the passage. He stretched out his other hand. Mick was trying to close a large penknife and he held it out to Harry. The handle behind Harry turned and the door burst open and threw him forward as he was taking the knife, which cut him. The boy grabbed the knife back. The policeman came into the room and Harry said, 'It's all right, I'm the welfare worker.' The policeman stood there. Harry was holding his wrist. The boy backed away. The scullery door suddenly opened and the woman with iron grey hair came out, moving like a bull. The boy got behind a chair. The woman came after him with her mouth in a thin line

26

and her shoulders forward. The boy ran into the scullery and slammed the door.

'He's cut 'im!' the woman shouted. Blood from Harry's hand dripped on the carpet. There was a cry from the yard and the man in gumboots came in quickly. He said "E's getting out of the window!' They all moved down the passage to the back door and saw an arm and a leg disappearing over a fence.

Harry shouted at the top of his voice 'Ring me, Mick, you know the number!'

Outside the porch where green leaves climbed amongst wrought iron railings and a stained-glass fanlight showed the bright colours of birds, a Rolls Royce drew up and unloaded first a chauffeur in a beige-coloured overcoat and cap and then, the door held open, a bowler-hatted figure head-on like a battering-ram. On the pavement this figure straightened itself into a dark-coated, gloved, umbrella'd man with a smooth brown face and silvering hair swept back at the sides in wings. He unbuttoned his overcoat and felt in the pockets of his waistcoat with his thumbs and forefingers, all the time smiling appreciatively up the street. He pulled a bunch of keys from a pocket and approached the door sorting them. The butler opened the door.

'Parks!'

"Morning, my lord.'

The butler took his hat and umbrella and gloves. On the hall table there was a pile of letters which he smoothed into a pack, fanned out, and selected two. They were addressed to THE RIGHT HON. LORD SYKES,

27

DSO. He took a small gold penknife from his waistcoat pocket and went to a window to try to open it.

He said 'Anyone with her ladyship?'

'Doctor Johnson has gone.'

Lord Sykes went up the stairs. His dark jacket had a single slit at the back which moved from side to side like the haunches of a horse. He stopped on the first landing and looked into an empty drawing-room, then went on. He put his head round the door of the bedroom with his pale blue eyes wrinkling. He said ''Ullo, 'ullo 'ullo!'

Lydia was sitting with her back to him at the dressing-table. She stretched her whitely made-up face at right angles. Lord Sykes approached and put his cheek down so that it was not quite touching hers. They made alternate sounds of kissing, like ping-pong bats.

'How was Malcom?'

'He sent you lots and lots – ' Lord Sykes was still trying to open his small gold penknife.

'Was Sid there?'

'No, Sid wasn't.'

'What is that?'

'A letter opener.'

'Let me do it.' Lydia took the penknife and bent over it. 'What did Malcom want?'

'Me!' Lord Sykes said. He made a mock-childish face.

Lydia fiddled with the knife. She said 'Harry was here this morning.'

'Harry Johnson?' Lord Sykes said.

Lydia dropped her hands in her lap and closed her eyes.

'The doctor, what?'

'My *brother* Harry,' Lydia said. Her shoulders shook. Then she went back to the knife. 'Harry Johnson!'

'Well if he changed his name from Bronstein he might have changed it to Harry, what?'

Lydia dropped her hands and closed her eyes again with exactly the same expression. Lord Sykes said '*Silly Benjy*' in his mock-childish voice. He laughed, making a clicking sound.

'He wanted to know about Annie Longley.'

'Don't we all,' Lord Sykes said.

'Have you heard?'

'The last I heard was when Jerril got a left and right with her and some other bird,' Lord Sykes said.

'You are disgusting,' Lydia said.

'What I want to know is how he does it,' Lord Sykes said. Lydia had opened the gold penknife and she handed it to him. He slit his letters with it. 'Does he line 'em up like a firing squad, what?'

'Please,' Lydia said.

'Or does he keep 'em in separate rooms and have 'em out in turn?' Lord Sykes was reading his letters.

Lydia went and stood by the picture like splintered glass and took a cigarette from a box. She said 'I don't think Harry knows about Jerril.'

Lord Sykes finished a letter and folded it. Lydia had her back to him. 'What?' he said.

'Oh it's useless!' Lydia said.

She was wearing a narrow black skirt with a white blouse above it. Lord Sykes suddenly lunged forwards and said 'Gnachh!' and pinched her behind.

'Benjy will you stop that!'

'*Naughty*,' Lord Sykes said. He did his high-pitched clicking laugh.

'You are a baby,' Lydia said. She went back to her dressing-table. She unscrewed a bottle and started putting varnish on her nails. She held her wrist out like the curved neck of a swan. She said 'Why wasn't Sid there?'

Harry sat in one of the adjustable armchairs opposite the woman with the iron-grey hairstyle. She gazed over his shoulder and chewed the inside of her lips steadily. He said 'Look, Mrs Jackson, you know at times you love him and at times you hate him, and you can't help it, can you?'

'If you say I've done anything wrong it's a lie,' the woman said.

'I'm not saying that, I'm saying it's normal,' Harry said.

'You said I hated him.'

'*You* said you hated him,' Harry said. He waited. 'When the policeman was here.'

The woman gazed above him through steel spectacles.

'You do get angry?' Harry said.

'When he gets a devil in him I hate him,' the woman said.

'All right,' Harry said. He sat forward smiling. 'He does get a devil in him. So in a way he can't help it. So who's going to help him?'

The woman said nothing.

'You can't. You're the closest person to him, so he takes it out on you. You know that, don't you?'

'I've been a good mother to him,' the woman said.

'Yes,' Harry said. He leaned back with his arms along the sides of the chair. 'But you can't stop getting angry sometimes. You try, but it's too difficult.'

'I do my best,' the woman said.

'I know,' Harry said.

'What can I do? He won't talk to me – ' The woman's strong, masculine face blurred suddenly with tears. 'He won't tell me where he's been. He hides things.'

'I know, Mrs Jackson.'

'I have to go out sometimes.'

Harry looked cautiously round the room: there was a clock on the mantelpiece but he could not see the hands.

'I don't go out much and then – ' The woman held a tiny handkerchief to her nose and turned her head away.

Harry waited.

'What'll happen to him?' the woman said. 'Where's he gone?'

'He'll come back,' Harry said.

'He cut you,' the woman said suddenly. She glared at him.

In the stillness there was the sound of distant, tinny music from a television set in the house next door. The woman began crying again.

'What do you want to happen to him?' Harry said.

'Can't you do something?'

'What?'

'They'll send him away,' the woman said. 'I only

31

wanted – ' She shook her head. 'He doesn't like me going out.'

'All right,' Harry said.

'I'm no use to him any more.' She pushed the handkerchief underneath her spectacles and held it there. 'I didn't want the police.'

'I think Mick should get away for a bit,' Harry said. 'Will you let me fix him up?'

'What's wrong – '

'A change would do you both good,' Harry said. 'Like a holiday. You're tired.'

The woman put her hands in her lap. 'Anyway where is he?'

'If he comes back here will you ring me?' Harry said. 'But I think he'll probably ring me first.'

'Where'll you put him?' the woman said.

'I'll find him a bed,' Harry said. He stood up. 'You needn't worry. I'll look after him.'

'I'm no use to him any more,' the woman said.

'It's not that,' Harry said. He noticed the hands of the clock, which said ten past one. 'He's fond of you; you are of him.' The tinny music came to a climax next door; there was the sound of guns firing. 'But the best you can do for him is to let him go for a while. Let him grow up.' Harry ran his hand through his hair. 'I'll see you tomorrow.'

The tears were running through the powder on the woman's face.

'It's no one's fault,' Harry said. 'I promise you.'

Annie climbed out of the taxi by a large office building

with a stone canopy projecting above the pavement. She went into a hall with a thick grey carpet and an enormous picture made of splintered glass. She waited for a lift. On an upper floor there was a passage with offices leading off like cubicles. Annie put her head round a door. She said 'Hullo,' brightly.

There was a girl behind a typewriter, and sitting on the desk a woman wearing skiing trousers and a thigh-length smock like a Russian. The woman said 'Annie come to see your Granny!' She took a cigarette-holder out of her mouth and put her cheek forward to be kissed. She said to the typist 'Put in that heading;' and to Annie 'How's my red-riding girl?'

'Very welly,' Annie said.

'You look waify,' the woman said. Her cigarette-holder was white with thin black bands round it. She turned to the typist. 'Doesn't she look waify?'

'I'm all right,' Annie said.

'Give the girl a drink,' the woman said. The typist took a bottle and two glasses from a filing cabinet. 'I thought you were on hol,' the woman said.

'Oh I am,' Annie said. She took the drink and sat down. 'I thought I'd see what was going on, you know?'

'Well nothing, luvvy. No handsome men or doggies in the rocket.'

'What is?' Annie said.

'Luvvy, bombs,' the woman said.

Annie sat holding the glass with her bright smile.

'You *are* waify. Come to tell Granny, hm?' She stood close to her. 'Mr Wolf, I know.'

Annie smiled.

33

'Such big teeth,' the woman said. She went to her desk and looked at a long strip of paper. 'But *which*?'

Annie said 'I know you're biz.'

'Can't get on without you luvvy.' The woman sucked on her holder. 'Look, give me a ring tomorrow, hm?'

'What are you doing?' Annie said.

'Sex murder. Moppets.' She pulled a photograph from a pile.

Annie said 'I saw a man like that this morning.'

'Your *friends*,' the woman said.

'You know how people come up the whole time, wanting to talk!' Annie laughed. The other two looked at her.

'Oh well,' Annie said. She stood up.

'Come back soon,' the woman said.

The telephone rang. The woman picked up the receiver. She said 'Put her through' and then 'Lyd–i–a!' She stood with her back to Annie. 'Yes' she said. 'Here. No.' She twirled the photograph round with her fingers. 'But very welly!'

She put her hand over the mouthpiece and turned to Annie. 'Ring me tomorrow, hm?'

Annie went out.

Jenny saw Harry coming through a glass door for the second time, and thought – *He was particularly dreadful to his wife*. Jenny was standing by the bar of a public house in which there were dozens of photographs of boxers on the walls. Harry looked round the crowded room and recognized Jenny. He unbuttoned his coat and began to feel in his pockets as if for a railway ticket.

34

Jenny stared at a sign which said *Restaurant* with an arrow pointing upwards.

Jenny wore a brown coat with a brown fur collar and black shoes. Harry raised his eyebrows and peered at a photograph of a boxer with *Good Times Geoff!* written across his legs. Jenny took a sip of gin and tonic and let it run into her mouth as if down a tube. Harry began moving towards the bar still groping in his pockets. Jenny breathed and her glass became misty. 'Oh hullo,' Harry said. 'Hullo,' Jenny said.

'Do you often come here?'

'Sometimes.'

'Would you like a drink?'

'Thanks.'

'I used to come here but I never do now,' Harry said.

Behind the bar were piles of cigarettes and small cigar packets. The barmaid wore a tight black skirt and no stockings. Ten shilling notes were stuck in a tumbler.

'Why not?' Jenny said.

'I don't know,' Harry said. He caught the attention of the barmaid and ordered a gin and tonic and a tomato juice. A corner of the brass moulding of the bar was bent back like a battery-terminal. He said 'There were burglar alarms ringing all the way in the street, why do they do that?'

'They have pre-arranged testing-times with the police,' Jenny said.

'How do you know?' Harry looked at her. She wore amber beads. Her hair and skin were honey-coloured.

'I read it somewhere,' Jenny said.

35

'I was looking for someone called Maurice Bloxham, do you know him?' Harry said.

'Yes, why do you want him?'

'Does he come here?'

'Yes,' Jenny said.

'You know everything,' Harry said. 'Can I ring you when I want things?'

Jenny took a sip. She had a peculiar way of swallowing as if the liquid washed straight through her. She said 'That would be exciting.'

Harry screwed his eyes up. He moved his head up and down as if he were listening to jazz. He looked down past the line of Jenny's hair to where her dark grey stockings were wrinkled above her ankles. Her black shoes were pointed.

A man came up behind Harry and put a hand on his shoulder. He said 'The fortnightly check-up, coming quietly?'

'Oh, Maurice,' Harry said. 'We were talking about you.'

'You were, were you?' Maurice said. He was wearing his brown suede jacket and tartan trousers. He looked at Jenny. He said 'And Jenny wren. What brought you back to your nest, Jenny?'

'Not the early worm,' Jenny said.

'You're so blunt,' Maurice said. He still had his hands on Harry's shoulder. 'Do you two know each other?'

'We've just met,' Harry said.

'Well I've got the low-down on him,' Maurice said. 'The truth that can be told.'

Harry said 'How's Annie, Maurice?'

'You'll be seeing her?'

'This evening probably.'

'I'll ring you,' Jenny said to Harry.

'That would be kind,' Harry said. He went out.

A boy of about eighteen with orange-coloured hair and a wrinkled face put his head round the door of the room where Helen was sitting. He smiled with his mouth in a surprised open 'O'. His expression seemed to have nothing to do with his sad eyes. Helen said 'Come in.' He looked round the room cautiously. Helen stopped typing.

'Can I help you?' Helen said.

'I was just wonderin' – ' the boy said. He stepped in. He stretched his fingers on each hand and placed the palms together in front of him. He clicked his tongue and spoke in a half-cockney and half-American accent. 'Know 'oo was on duty 'ere last night?'

'On the telephone?' Helen said. 'What time?'

''Bout twelve,' the boy said.

Helen opened a book like a ledger. She ran her finger up and down. 'Mr Gates' she said. 'Harry Gates.'

'Harry Gates, eh?' The boy bounced the palms of his hands together. 'Coming in today?'

'I expected him at lunch, but I'm afraid he's not here yet.'

The boy nodded.

'He should be in if you'd like to wait.'

The boy clicked his tongue again. He leaned at an angle as if about to fall over. 'Don't think I will, thanks.'

'Take a chair,' Helen said. She looked at the ledger. 'Did you speak to Mr Gates last night?'

'Oh, ah – ' the boy said. He peered round.

'May I have your name – your Christian name?'

The boy bent down suddenly and looked at a book-case. 'Jules,' he said.

'Jewels,' Helen said. She wrote it down. She followed where the boy was looking and saw a row of bound magazines called *Living London*.

The boy lurched towards the door. His face split into a smile like the opening of a gladstone bag.

'Are you sure you won't – ?' Helen said.

The boy sighed. He scratched his head. His hair was in a fringe with ragged edges. He went out.

Beside the statue of Richard Cœur de Lion the Rolls Royce drew up and unloaded first the chauffeur in beige uniform and then, the door held open, the bowler-hatted figure head-on like a battering-ram. On the pavement Lord Sykes straightened himself and felt in his waist-coat pockets all the time smiling appreciatively up the street. There was a small queue next door waiting to go into the House of Commons. Lord Sykes moved towards the door behind the statue in the façade of the huge pinnacled building. A policeman saluted him and he said 'Constable!' and a doorman saluted him and he said 'Hopkins!' The doorman said "Afternoon, my Lord.'

Inside the House of Lords there was a low vaulted gallery with innumerable hooks for clothes. A footman helped him off with his coat and hat and hung them beneath a label which said *Lord Sykes, DSO*. He moved down the middle of the gallery on a red carpet with the slit at the back of his jacket undulating slightly. He held his hands half in and half out of his pockets with his thumbs forwards. His blue eyes wrinkled.

He went up some stairs and along a passage with panelled walls on either side. A tall thin bishop in gaiters was coming towards him and stood to one side to let him pass. The bishop swayed slightly like blown paper.

Down some more steps and through a pointed gothic door Lord Sykes entered a room furnished with leather chairs and leather-inlaid furniture and a white lamp-bowl hanging from the ceiling by chains. An old man sat in one of the chairs. He had white hair and a bright red face. He was reading a newspaper. Lord Sykes closed the door. The old man put the paper down. Lord Sykes went to the desk and put his fingers on it. The old man said 'What did Malcom say?'

'I hope you haven't been waiting long,' Lord Sykes said.

'It's what we thought?'

'Yes.'

'Why's it secret?'

'It's not.' Lord Sykes sat behind the desk and pulled a bunch of keys from his waistcoat pocket. There was a dispatch-box in front of him.

'They've done everything with publicity before,' the old man said. He had small black eyes bedded in his face like truffles.

'The publicity they wanted.'

'Do we know what they've left out?'

Lord Sykes unlocked the dispatch-box. He said 'Well we couldn't, could we?'

The old man said 'Haven't we got intelligence?' He had a way of opening his lips with his teeth closed so that his mouth was an uneven 'O'.

'Malcom is getting information.'

'Good God!' He seemed to be shouting at someone deaf. 'Are we crazy?'

Lord Sykes took some papers from the dispatch-box, locked it, put the key in his waistcoat pocket, and stood up. He said 'Coming?'

The old man said 'I haven't been in this place thirty years.'

'See if it's improved,' Lord Sykes said.

The old man struggled to his feet with the help of a rubber-tipped walking-stick. They went along a stone-flagged passage. The old man put his hand on Lord Sykes's arm. They stopped. 'What does it mean?' he said. Lord Sykes smiled. They emerged in a huge hall like Euston Station. There were men in groups leaning inwards and talking. Their eyes went off at tangents. An impersonal hum filled the room.

'How can we not know?' the old man shouted.

They went through glass doors which led into a high panelled chamber with red leather benches on either side and a gallery and stained-glass windows above. There was a golden throne at the far end and in front of it a man in a wig with his hands on his knees. Microphones hung by wires from the ceiling. On the benches there were men sitting and half lying and some holding earphones. A man in black knee-breeches and

42

carrying a stick stood by the door. A man with smooth parted hair like a boxer was making a speech. He said '. . . the story of the psychiatrist who showed a man an ink blot and asked him what it was.'

'What is this?' the old man said.

'Mental Health,' Lord Sykes whispered.

The man with the knee-breeches turned and put a finger to his lips.

' "A horse?" the man said,' the man with smooth parted hair said. There was a low murmur from the benches.

The old man reached over a bench in front of him and picked up an earphone. He said 'How does this thing work?'

The man with knee-breeches whispered 'Please be quiet.'

The man with smooth parted hair said 'He showed him another one. "A horse," the man said'. There was another murmur from the benches. It sounded like – yeah, yeah.

The old man was struggling with his earphones. 'Get an electrician,' he said loudly. The man in knee-breeches tried to take it away. The old man dragged it back.

'Why? "Because everything reminds me of a horse",' the man with smooth parted hair said.

The murmur from the audience rose to a rumbling.

'Let me out of here,' the old man shouted. He banged through the swing doors.

Lord Sykes remained standing just inside, leaning

slightly forward, his hands in his jacket pockets, thumbs outside, his blue eyes smiling.

Annie leaned with her back against a parapet above the river. In front of her long lines of traffic stood shaking. There was a bridge on her left along which heads of people were moving. There were people coming down the hill opposite her and winding through a garden past an empty bandstand and the statue of a poet. There were people coming up the road dodging between the traffic and merging into the queues waiting for buses. People came down the steps from the bridge zigzagging and joining the crowds at the bottom and converging on the entrance of an underground station. There were men shouting and waving newspapers like flags. The sky was a deep violet colour with a yellowish light on the buildings. A clock boomed in the distance. More people came down the hill. They were shaken into the streets like dust.

Annie pirouetted and looked at the river. It was opaque with yellow reflections. The crowds going into the underground were spreading out in tunnels beneath the water. They were moving in long lines along white-tiled passages. The river ran on a bed of broken iron.

Annie stretched her face as if there was a wind. Behind her, she put one foot behind the other with a toe pointing towards the ground. She hummed. There seemed to be a separation between the two halves of her body; the top stretching over the reflections like

44

quicksilver, and the bottom immersed in the swarming crowds.

In the distance the violet sky flashed. There was a rush of birds past her head. The air went dark and a line of rain came bouncing up the river like bullets. The thunder burst. In quietness, the rain hissed.

Annie looked round. The crowds lit by the yellow lights of the underground station appeared above the surface of the water as if they were already in it, immersing themselves with the ones at the back pushing until they disappeared. There was a scream of starlings above their heads. The rain turned to hail, falling like tracers.

There was a narrow junction between the two halves of her body towards which a trickle of water approached from her neck. She leaned on her back, her elbows on the parapet, on tiptoe. The trickle of water was like a snake, with the next flash of thunder. She held her breath. The snake crept round her waist and settled there. The figures in the outside world had ceased. The landscape was white. A crowd of ghostly figures seemed to rush up from her body and disappear into the evening like flames.

Harry came into the room where Helen was sitting and said 'I've walked, I had to leave the car.' 'What an evening!' Helen said. Harry sat down in the rickety chair by the gas fire. 'You look tired,' Helen said.

Harry said 'I got to Mick Jackson and it was going all right, then someone sent for the police, the neighbours I think, Mrs Jackson was yelling. Mick disappeared but

45

he'll turn up, probably ring here, you did say he knew the number?'

'Yes,' Helen said.

'I told him to ring, I was getting along o.k., I'll take it when he does. This afternoon I saw the police and it's all right with them, and I saw the hostel and Charlie will take him. The thing is to get him away from mum.'

'What have you done to your hand?' Helen said.

'Mick had a knife and between us we dropped it, like a farce,' Harry said.

'It's all right?'

'Yes.' Harry tipped his chair back. He had his hands in his pockets. He said 'Have there been any other calls for me, I mean Mick hasn't rung yet?'

Helen said. 'There was one other.'

'Oh there was?' Harry blushed.

'From your sister. She was reminding you you were having dinner there tonight.'

'Oh blast,' Harry said.

'Did you expect any others?'

'No,' Harry said.

'Then there was that man Bill you saw last night, he called in.'

'What did he want?'

'Money, really.' Helen moved papers about on the desk. 'Did you give him some last night?'

'Yes,' Harry said.

'I don't know, Harry, but I wonder if that will help them, I mean people will come and expect nothing else.'

'One never knows what will help,' Harry said. He stretched his legs, tipping the chair back farther.

'Anyway I told him about cheaper lodgings and assistance, and said come back after I'd talked to you.'

'I only gave him two pounds' Harry said. 'He might need it even if he was trying it on.'

'But you know the trouble with the accounts.'

'Oh the accounts!' Harry said.

Helen adjusted the typewriter. She took some sheets of paper, separated them, put carbon paper in between, shuffled the lot together and wound them in.

Harry said 'Sorry, Helen, anything else?'

'Well there was a strange boy, about eighteen, he said he'd spoken to you last night, but I couldn't find it in the book.'

'Last night,' Harry said. He rocked backwards and forwards.

'About midnight.'

'No, it was quiet. There was only one call, from a friend. A woman,' he added. He tipped the chair forward. 'He couldn't have been anything to do with that?'

'He said his name was Jewels,' Helen said.

'Jewels!' Harry said. He stretched his eyes dramatically.

Helen looked at him. The bandage round his wrist was coming unravelled. His collar was undone. She said 'You're not going to your sister's are you? You haven't had much sleep.'

Harry said 'I've got to wait for Mick. I might as well wait there.' He sat hunched with his legs under the chair. 'If he rings, could you or whoever's on take the message and say that I'll come and pick him up wherever he is. Tell him just to stay there. Then ring me at my sister's.'

'I can pick him up,' Helen said.

'I'd rather,' Harry said. 'I did it badly this morning.'

'I'm sure you didn't,' Helen said.

'Besides, if he rings up late it'll be no good for the hostel tonight, and I'll have to take him home.' He balanced himself again like someone on a trapeze.

'Don't overdo it,' Helen said.

'I'm not tired,' Harry said. 'I'm just not right for this job.'

Helen typed a few words with two fingers. 'Why not?'

'I'm a poet,' Harry said. 'Did you ever read any of my poems, Helen?'

'I'm afraid not,' Helen said.

'You're lucky,' Harry said. He was almost horizontal. 'Though this job's like a poem, you don't know what you're doing you just do it.'

'You go home and get cleaned up,' Helen said.

'But I mean – ' Harry said. He put his head back 'Here we are, trying – ' His chair almost went over backwards. He lurched with one hand to the ground. Helen put her head in her hands and laughed. Harry slid to the floor.

'Go on,' Helen said.

Harry looked up. 'But you will let me know?'

'Yes,' Helen said.

'You'll put any other messages through to my sister's?'

'Yes,' Helen said.

'There is one other I'm expecting,' Harry said.

* * *

48

Father Patterson sat in a room furnished with nothing but bed, wash-stand, chest of drawers, table, chair, linoleum, and crucifix. He was dressed in an overcoat and muffler. He had a rug round his legs and wore one glove. Beside him on the floor was a small electric fire, out, with its grey face turned up like a dog. He was writing on a yellow sheet of lined paper. He wrote –

The fall of man into not evil but helplessness.
A world which appears to have no meaning.
The need to know the area within which meaning is experienced.

When there is no meaning it is like a car out of gear: the engine moves but to no effect.
When there is meaning this is experienced as movement in relation to the things outside it.
What is the action that puts the car in gear?
The need to know the point at which free will operates.

Father Patterson looked at his watch. It was three minutes to seven. He put down his pen, unwrapped his legs, took off his gloves and coat, went out, down two flights of stone stairs, and into a room on the ground floor. It was a chapel. There was no one else in it. He struck a match, lit two candles on the altar, sat in a choir-stall facing inwards, picked up two books and marked places in them, laid them on a shelf in front of him, knelt, stood up, bowed to the altar, sat down again, read for five minutes, changed books, crossed his legs, read again, stood up, looked at the ceiling for a bit, sat down, read again, turned to the altar, bowed, knelt, stayed with his head on his hands for ten minutes, stood up, snuffed the candles, genuflected, and went out.

Upstairs in his room he wrote –

A point: theoretically of no magnitude; but without which magnitude has no meaning.

If we try to influence magnitude directly, we fail. We have to work at the centre, by which the circumference is affected.

Free will lies only at a single point.

How, in a position of no dimension, can there be a choice?

He looked at the window. The thunder had passed into the distance with occasional booming. There were the outlines of chimneys and television aerials black against the sky.

He wrote –

A point which has dimension is that of God.

Choice within this is first in recognizing it exists; then in facing it; then in trusting its efficacy.

The centre moves. Everything else moves with it.

Not an engine: but a sail catching the wind.

You tighten a rope: a life keels over.

There is excitement; danger.

A universe.

* * *

'But what's the point of it?' Lord Sykes said. 'We've got the police, haven't we?'

'Why do you think he will ring up?' Lydia said.

'What else can he do?' Harry said.

They were round a table of silver spoons and coffee-cups. Lydia wore a velvet dress with a pink turban on her head. Lord Sykes was in a wine-coloured jacket. Harry sat with his hands turned inwards under his thighs.

'I mean,' Harry said, 'he can't go home, he can't stay out all night, so he'll either break in somewhere or ring up.'

'Why won't he break in?'

'He might,' Harry said.

The butler entered with glasses and a bottle. Harry shook his head. Lord Sykes took brandy. Lydia unwrapped a chocolate.

'Let me get this,' Lord Sykes said. 'The boy's got a knife, he's already attacked his mother, he's wounded you, he's run away from the police, he's been out on the streets all day, he may break in, yet there's no one out there looking for him, the police have been stopped, and you're waiting for him to ring up.'

'Benjy – ' Lydia said.

'Isn't that so?' Lord Sykes said.

'But it's not like that,' Harry said. 'It only matters if someone does the wrong thing now.'

'Which is what?'

'Mucks him up,' Harry said.

Lord Sykes raised his eyebrows, took a cigar, turned it round, sucked at it.

'He's probably been in a cinema all day,' Harry said. 'He'll ring up when he gets out at ten past ten.'

'Why d'you think he's in a cinema?' Lydia said.

'What would you do?' Harry said. 'Look – ' He did his gesture of running his hand through his hair. 'He's not a bad boy, he's in a mess with his mother, his father hopped it. So his mother goes out with the lodger. Well, why shouldn't she?' Lydia stared at him. 'But the boy minds. Nothing wrong with that. But the mother knows. So she nags him, in two rooms, with a voice that you could hear all over Buckingham Palace. So he panics. She's as big as a bull. What would you do?'

'Me?' Lydia said. She crossed her arms in front of her velvet gown.

'So you haven't got anything against the police,' Lord Sykes said.

'No,' Harry said.

'You don't say your methods are right and theirs wrong, but both have their normal function in society.'

'We're tiny,' Harry said. 'We can just help get this one boy away.'

'And that's what you want,' Lord Sykes said.

Harry went on – 'Or if we can't, or if he does break in somewhere, that doesn't matter either, he may have to learn that way. What matters is there's always some-one to help him.'

'Hard luck for the person he breaks in on, though,' Lord Sykes said.

'Yes,' Harry said.

He looked round the room. There were Dutch land-scapes of two-thirds sky and the rest flat fields with trees. There was a clock with a silver bell on it that had been in his and Lydia's home as children.

Lord Sykes said 'You want the best of it both ways. What if he killed someone?'

Harry said 'That would be hard luck on me, wouldn't it?'

Lydia stood up. They followed her out of the dining-room. On the way to the first floor Lord Sykes put his hand on Harry's arm and said 'Good luck if I don't see you!' He went on up the stairs.

In a small room with yellow curtains and red-and-silver striped chairs Lydia sat with her feet curled up. Harry stood with one elbow on the mantelpiece and his wrist at the back of his neck. He said 'Now I feel dreadful!'

'I don't know why,' Lydia said.

'What I should have said is that you must trust. Of course it's stupid if you don't.'

'Trust what?' Lydia said.

'Everything,' Harry said. Then – 'Did you find Annie?'

'I rang her office and spoke to Granny Dooland, Annie was all right.'

'Who?' Harry said.

'Pansy Dooland,' Lydia said. 'Did you know Annie was having an affair with Jerril?'

'Jerril?' Harry said. He stretched his eyes affectedly. 'But I thought Jerril – I mean – I saw him last night.'

'How?' Lydia said.

'But this doesn't make sense,' Harry said. He rubbed his head. 'Look – Jerril was having dinner last night with a girl. At lunch I met Maurice who seemed to be with Annie – I mean, he'd seen her this morning. Then Maurice said – I think he said – he'd waited for this girl – and he stayed with her at lunch. Then this evening with Annie. And Annie's with Jerril?' He bent towards Lydia. 'That's wonderful!'

'She was in the office,' Lydia said.

'Isn't it?' Harry said. He walked up and down. 'What a mess!'

'Who was the girl?' Lydia said.

'She said she'd ring me,' Harry said. 'Now why did she say that?'

'Who?' Lydia said.

'She said she'd find out where Annie was. You see – because of Jerril? or Maurice?' He stopped.

'Are you still in love with Annie?' Lydia said.

Harry said 'No.'

'Well, you're well out of it then.'

'Yes I am,' Harry said. He stood still, appearing to listen.

'Who was the girl?'

'Everyone sometimes wants to get back in,' Harry said.

The butler came to the door and said 'Mr Harry, there's a call with two messages for you'.

Harry drove through North London along the cobbles of old tramlines. There were the lighted windows of shops in patches, the buildings on either side became lower until the sky seemed to lie above ruins. Harry held a street-map in front of him. He zigzagged, losing the kerb. He stopped beneath a streetlight.

The inside of the car was lit in patches. The heater whirred. He switched off the engine and the noise died. The map had a large green area with a pond in it. He drove on.

Beside a heath where the darkness was flat on the ground he came to a lighted call-box and stopped. A figure came out of the shadows. He opened the door and said 'Jump in, Mick.' The boy climbed in beside him. Harry said 'Have you had any trouble?' The boy said 'No.' Harry started back the way he had come. He said 'You can spend the night at my home, we'll fix things in the morning.'

The boy sat beside him like an animal kept warm by old clothes. Harry glanced at him in the passing light and his cheek was delicate as a girl's. Harry said 'Did you go to a film?' 'I saw a picture,' the boy said 'What was it?' '*The Brothers Karamazov*,' the boy said. 'It's a very good book,' Harry said.

They crossed a bridge over railway lines. The boy sat with his head hunched forwards. His hair stuck up making a halo above his forehead. He said 'Is this a Consul?' 'Yes,' Harry said. He ran a hand through his hair. '1958?' the boy said. 'I think so,' Harry said.

They came to a crossroads. Harry said 'Have you had anything to eat?'

'It doesn't matter.'

'We'll find a café.' Harry turned along a well-lighted street with dummies in the windows of dark-skinned girls with pale pink eyes and lips. There was a beach scene of a girl on her back and a man with golden hair and a gold moustache above her. Harry said 'I can never think where will be open' He thought – *Where shall we go? and she, You decide.* He smiled. There was a peculiar contraption of unlighted bulbs of a figure holding an orb and a sceptre floating above the road. *Why don't we go home? she said.* He said to the boy 'Somewhere here.'

They stopped by a neon sign of a goose with a large yellow egg. Inside there were red-topped tables with wooden chairs and a counter with sandwiches and soft-drink cylinders. Harry said. 'What would you like?' 'Pork chops and french fried potatoes,' the boy said.

There was a staircase going down at the far end with a notice saying *Members Only*. From below came the thump of a juke-box and a record of a boy's voice crying in an echo-chamber. The room had strip lighting which made skin look a yellowish green. The boy's food arrived in a mountain of potatoes and peas. Harry drank coffee.

Two girls came in wearing short white mackintoshes belted at the waist. Their hair sat on their heads like huge spiders, one dark red and the other white. They had small brown faces and silver lips and eyelids. They carried umbrellas. They began spinning round in time to the music, holding their wrists out like the necks of swans.

Two boys wearing heavy hooped jerseys and tight trousers came in and slammed the door behind them and walked to the head of the stairs each with a movement of stuffing a comb in his back hip pocket. The girls followed.

Mick said 'They don't know how to do a chop.'

Mick's jacket was of a black material that seemed to be crumbling. Harry had the impression of sacking in a gardener's hut with something white inside. There was fair hair on Mick's cheek just in front of his ear. Harry said 'I used to come to places like this, but I never do now.'

Mick said 'I work in a kitchen.'

'They've got dancing downstairs,' Harry said.

'I don't do it,' Mick said.

'I used to,' Harry said. 'I used quite to fancy myself at it.'

Mick looked at him. Their eyes met for a moment; then went away. Harry said 'Do you work tomorrow?'

'Not Saturdays.' Mick said.

Harry said 'Good. Let's go home.'

They drove along the main road and turned into quiet streets with houses in small blocks with gardens. Harry stopped in front of a semi-detached house of two storeys with gables. He said 'Here.' He walked through a small garden and up some steps. The boy followed him. Harry said 'You can have my son's room, he's away at school.' Inside there was a carpeted hall with a staircase going up. On the first floor a door opened on to a small room with a divan bed and a cactus on a table and a model of the Taj Mahal. Harry took a pair of pyjamas and threw them on the bed and said 'Try these.' The boy began undressing. 'The bathroom's next door,' Harry said. He turned on a switch by the bed which lit up the model of the Taj Mahal. The boy put on the pyjama jacket. 'All right?' Harry said. 'Yes,' the boy said. He went to the washbasin and turned the tap on. 'Good night,' Harry said.

* * *

In the middle of the night Harry sat up in bed violently. There was the sensation of machinery at the top of his palate and just behind his eyes – a grinding of huge cog-wheels turning. The noise went slowly outwards into the darkness and became quiet. He lowered his head, breathing deeply. His eyes drooped. Then he seemed to feel a rush of air behind him and the blade of a guillo-tine, horizontal, swinging to cut off his head. He fell sideways like someone kicked. He lay half out of the bedclothes and groaned. He had an impression of soft white skin and sacking. He swivelled over the edge of the bed so that he was kneeling. He stretched and felt for the light.

He blinked one eye against the glare until the bed-room came into view with its pale and rather feminine-looking furniture and fitted carpet and large double bed. He got out of bed and went to the washbasin and took a bottle of pills and a glass of water. Holding these, he opened the door on to the landing and listened.

He sat on the edge of the bed again and drifted into a daydream. He was in a room with Annie, walking up and down. He was talking. He said 'What else could I have done?' He woke with a jump and undid the bottle and tipped two pills into his hand and swallowed them with water. He got into bed and sat upright and read a book. After a few sentences he switched the light off.

There was an ache in the lower part of his chest and the whirring of cog-wheels again somewhere outside him. He lay and tried to let his mind slip away but when he thought about it it came back. He thought of horses jumping and they floated towards him in slow motion. The ache, or wound, was in the dark outside him. He imagined goblins with rubber faces: a headless man. Then, from nowhere, he felt himself cutting his own throat. He jumped up and said 'Oh God!' He swivelled on to his knees again and began to pray 'Christ have mercy on us.' He repeated this. He was curled in a ball with his head down by his knees. After a while, he straightened himself before he went to sleep.

Annie woke with the impression that there was someone trying to climb in at her window. She switched on the light and went in her nightdress and drew the curtains and saw Jerril's head outside on a level with the lower sill. The window hung from sash-cords but the edges had been painted over and it would not move. An air-conditioner bulged at one side of it. Annie went to a small kitchen next door and opened the window and put her head out. Jerril had his elbows on the ledge of the bedroom window and one foot on a fire-escape some distance away. The other foot hung in front of a window on the floor below. His toe scraped the air. Annie took a mop and held it out to him. Jerril let go with his foot on the fire-escape and it swung beside the other one and crashed through the glass of the window below. He struggled on to his hands. Annie let the mop fall, and it floated down in the darkness. There was another crash of glass. Annie went back to the bedroom.

Jerril was sitting outside on the window ledge with his arms round the bulge of the air-conditioner. The ledge was wide enough for him to be out of sight from below. There was a shout in the courtyard and the noise of a window opening. The protruding end of the air-conditioner was in Jerril's lap and his arms were above it like someone holding a guitar. Annie put a finger to her lips. Jerril made a face and began strumming on the air-conditioner. Annie laughed. She put her ear down to the inside grill which was like a wireless. She switched on the air-conditioner and it wheezed into life. Jerril made a startled face and then pretended to put a stethoscope in his ears and take soundings on the air-conditioner. He laid two fingers on it and tapped. Annie doubled up with laughter. There were voices below and a torch shone upwards. Footsteps came up the stairs and approached along the passage. Jerril was playing on the air-conditioner and his mouth opened and shut as if in a passionate song. Annie was laughing so much that she had to kneel and bury her face in the bed. There was silence; then the footsteps in the passage went away.

Father Patterson sat on the parapet of a fountain in Trafalgar Square. He looked over the heads of a large crowd in the morning light. On the plinth of the statue a man was making a speech. There were about thirty people on the platform – pale men in mackintoshes, some Japanese in blue overcoats, two Indian women in saris, a negro in a sports jacket, a very tall woman with a feather in her hair. The speaker was a short spectacled Englishman who held his head close to the microphone and spoke in rhythmic phrases.

'Even as we stand there are circling round us these engines that can destroy us, destroy us not only city by city or country by country but totally and for ever. Even as we stand there is one man – for in the end it is always one man – who can either destroy us or not destroy us. And it is not just ourselves who are destroyed, not our homes and all that has made life dear to us; it is our children and our children's children and the whole race of man for ever.'

He spoke with his head on one side and his eyes gazing into the distance. He paused and licked his lips and leaned forwards again. The crowd listened. There were families with babies in push-chairs; mothers with scarves round their heads; fathers with caps and mufflers; old men with wrinkled faces and boys and girls with untidy hair. Their faces were nearly all *good*, Father Patterson thought – faces that had once appeared in religious art.

A woman in thigh-length smock and black trousers came bicycling through the traffic at the far end of the square and bumped on to the pavement and freewheeled round the back of the crowd. She was followed by a small newspaper van with a banner across its roof saying just PANSY DOOLAND. It pulled up at the curb and two men got out carrying cameras. The woman rolled along to a group of policemen where she stopped and leaned on her handlebars. An officer holding a pair of gloves smiled at her and hit the gloves against his other hand.

Close to Father Patterson there was a group, mostly young, standing round a banner between two poles which said FROM FEAR TO SANITY. Holding one pole was a man in tartan trousers and a brown suede jacket. At the back of the group was a girl in a brown coloured coat with a brown fur collar and honey-coloured hair.

The man on the platform shouted 'Is there one of us who thinks himself a God to hold this power?'

Coming trundling down the hill past the National Gallery was another enclosed van with small barred windows. It went round the square and pulled up outside South Africa House. Stationary, it rocked on its springs and a chanting came from inside. A short fat man in a leather coat got out of the front seat and went to open the door at the back. He clanked an iron bar and stood to one side. A dozen men came out and ran towards the fountain. They unfurled a banner between two poles which said CAMERON IS COMING.

The man on the platform finished his speech. A clergyman stepped to the microphone and said 'I am now going to ask Jerril Muller, the well-known artist, to read a poem he has written for the occasion.' Jerril stepped forward. He was wearing his grey suit and dark blue shirt. He said –

>At the end man destroyed heaven and earth
>The earth with living things that move
>And love, and have their dominion
>Over death and you my child

In front of the group beneath the banner saying CAMERON IS COMING was a boy with orange hair and curiously wrinkled skin. He put his hands to his mouth and shouted 'Moo moo Muller,' with a noise like a cow. The man in the suede jacket holding the banner saying

FROM FEAR TO SANITY shouted 'Quiet!' The man in the leather coat walked quickly to the front of the CAMERON IS COMING group and began conducting them in a song. They sang –

> We're going to fight for freedom
> For freedom and for home

to the tune of 'Home Sweet Home'. They made swinging gestures with their fists.

The man in the suede jacket began leading his group towards them round the edge of the fountain. The other group were opening and shutting their mouths but making little noise against Jerril and the loudspeakers. The man in the suede jacket had arrived next to them and he lowered his banner which said FROM FEAR TO SANITY so that it tangled in the banner which said CAMERON IS COMING. The four poles jostled like giant diabolo sticks. The lower banner was heaved upwards dragging the top one out of the hands of its bearers. The man in the suede jacket and the man in the leather coat began fighting. They held their fists high and punched each other on the forearms. The boy with orange hair was attacked by two smaller men: he defended himself clumsily, his mouth pursed in a curious open 'O'.

Jerril was going on with his poem.

> Crowds that run to water and the water fire
> Blood that turns to heaven and the heaven hell
> Shouts in silence; the falling stars
> And the earth is air.

The fighting broke up, stopped, started again. Men walked round and took short runs at each other. People were trying to disentangle the two banners. Policemen walked through the crowd and began moving the two groups to the side of the square. The man in the leather coat said 'May I ask under what statute . . . ?' A policeman pushed him. The man in the suede jacket shouted 'That's my property!' A photographer took a picture of the girl in the brown coat. An officer said 'Keep moving.' The man in the leather coat put his head down and took a run at the police and was caught and turned round and lifted by his elbows. He was carried with his arms akimbo, smiling. The boy with orange hair had circled round the police and came and sat next to Father Patterson. He dabbed at his nose. The others were pushed outside the rampart on the side of the square. Father Patterson said 'What are you?'

Jules said 'Eh?' and then – 'National Defence.'

'What are you trying to do?'

'Oh – ' Jules said. He had spoken in his deep drawl, but now switched to his half-American, half-cockney. 'Doing the niggers and yids, y'know.'

'You think it's a joke?' Father Patterson said.

'Oh not a *joke*,' Jules said.

Father Patterson looked towards the plinth. Jerril had finished, and people clapped. The clergyman announced a march down Whitehall. Father Patterson's face went flat and tired.

Jules rubbed his hands up and down on his thighs. He said 'You interested in politics?'

'Yes,' Father Patterson said.

'Someone's got to fight.'

'Why this?' Father Patterson waved his hand at the group beyond the rampart who had formed up again and were opening and shutting their mouths in unison.

'For the giggle,' Jules said.

The crowd had drifted to the south side of the square. Pansy Dooland balanced on her bicycle with her legs out. A policeman pushed her. A flock of pigeons fluttered down and pecked on the ground.

'What do you want to do with your life?' Father Patterson said.

'Oh –' Jules said. It was like a roar, or a groan. He scratched his head. 'What would I do with my life!'

'If you had the chance,' Father Patterson said.

Jules screwed his face up. 'We didn't have the war.'

'You like fighting?'

Jules's face moved like a bag being open and shut. 'I know it's childish.'

The crowd had moved away leaving them alone on the fountain. The girl with the brown coat and honey-coloured hair wandered across the square alone and went into a telephone box. Jules rocked backwards and forwards with his hands on his thighs. Father Patterson sat hunched in his black cassock. A thin sun shone in their eyes.

'You see,' Jules said in his deep voice; 'It's a matter of the will. Against foreigners, I suppose. These people –' he waved his hand at the empty square ' – they mind dying!' He said this with great scorn. 'I don't. Truly!'

'That's all right,' Father Patterson said. He took a

notebook out of his cassock and tore off a leaf and began writing on it.

'But what *for*,' Jules said, 'I don't know.'

Father Patterson held out the piece of paper. 'This is my address. Come and see me.'

'Oh thanks' Jules said. He blushed. He wiped his hands on his trousers before he took the paper.

Father Patterson said, 'Lunch tomorrow.'

'Oh well!' Jules said.

The police were walking across the square. They had been laughing and talking, but when they passed Father Patterson and Jules they became silent and looked at the ground.

From a window in the Foreign Office Lord Sykes watched the small crowd of marchers who had reached Downing Street and there had been stopped by the police. There had been an argument between the leaders of the group and an officer, and the marchers had sat down. They stretched round the entrance to the street and up the pavement in Whitehall. They sat cross-legged, with their arms round their knees.

In the room with Lord Sykes was a young fair-haired man wearing a dark suit with a single slit in the jacket and a blue-and-white striped shirt with a white collar and yellow tie. He stood by Lord Sykes and said 'I thought they'd got over sitting on their bottoms.'

'Still wet behind their rears,' Lord Sykes said.

'Oh!' the young man cried.

A wind blew through the hair of the seated crowd. A child stumbled over their legs. Pansy Dooland came free-wheeling down Whitehall and crossed the road standing on one pedal.

Lord Sykes put his hand on the young man's shoulder. He rocked him backwards and forwards. With his other hand he held a cigarette-holder in his mouth and sucked. The smile on the young man's face had become fixed showing large white teeth.

The room they were in was an office with a leather-topped desk and leather chairs and a light in a white bowl hanging from the ceiling. There was a faded red carpet with a flowered border. Lord Sykes said 'There's Maurice Bloxham, what?'

The young man said 'With those girls with hair all over their eyes?'

'What I want to know,' Lord Sykes said, 'is how he does it.' He took his hand off the young man's shoulder.

A clock began striking. Traffic slowed in the road outside. Lord Sykes went to the desk. He said 'What are you doing tomorrow? I wonder if you'd like to come to the country, Lydia's having one of her gatherings.' He was putting papers into a briefcase.

'I'd adore it,' the young man said.

Lord Sykes strapped up the briefcase. He went back to the window. He said 'You'd like it, what?'

The young man bit on his lower lip and put his head on one side. He had bright blue eyes. His hair was corn-coloured.

Lord Sykes sucked on his holder. In the street more police had arrived. They formed a line. Lord Sykes said 'I could pick you up. About eleven-thirty?'

'That is so sweet,' the young man said.

67

Lord Sykes swayed on his toes. He squeezed the young man's arm. Then he went out of the room and down a wide stone staircase and across a courtyard into Downing Street. He stood on the pavement behind the line of police and buttoned his coat and tapped his cigarette-holder on his knuckles. He called out to a policeman 'Officer!' and the policeman said 'Morning, Lord Sykes, fine day for the mudlarks!' Lord Sykes said 'Still wet behind their rears, what?'

He went in the opposite direction, into St James's Park, adjusting the buttons of his overcoat. His blue eyes were wrinkled at the corners. In the park there were children throwing bread to the ducks. A pelican stretched his huge beak to scratch beneath its wing.

Jules went into a pub at the back of Trafalgar Square and saw the man in the leather coat who had been with him in the square. The man had one elbow on the bar and a foot on the bottom rail. He said 'Where did you get?' Jules said 'Doubled back and had a sit-down by the fountain.' The man said 'That was a bloody help.' 'Did you win the war?' Jules said.

He stood by the man, the top of whose head came up to his shoulder. The man had a yellowish round face with a Hitler moustache. He shuffled his foot along the rail so that he was close to Jules. He said 'You want to watch it.' 'What, you?' Jules said. 'Try?' the man said.

There was a wireless behind the bar giving police announcements. The voice said 'The police are looking for a man who may be able to help them in their inquiries into the murder of an eight-year-old girl in Regent's

Park last week. He is of medium height, greying hair, reddish complexion. . . .'

There was a group of three strangers at the bar. One of them said 'They should 'ave 'is balls off before they hang 'im.' Jules turned to the stranger and said 'Oh you don't want to hurt 'im, do you?' The three men stared at him. ''E was just 'avin a bit o' fun,' Jules said.

'Are you serious?' one of the strangers said.

'Course I am,' Jules said. He spoke in his elaborate mock-cockney. 'All me sympathies is with the murderer an' none wiv the victim, 'aven't you 'eard of people like me?'

The man in the leather coat put his arm round Jules. He said 'All right then.'

'I'm an intellectual,' Jules said. He tapped his head. 'I'm sick, in here. Not a criminal.'

'You sod off,' one of the strangers said.

The man in the leather coat had both arms round Jules as if he were trying to lift him. Jules leaned forward.

'We've all got to love one another,' Jules said. 'It says so, doesn't it?' He began jerking up and down in the arms of the man who held him.

One of the strangers lifted a hand as if to hit him. The man in the leather coat let go and came round in front with his arms up. He grabbed the stranger by the sleeve. The stranger punched at him. They all began fighting with Jules leaning over the head of the man in the leather coat with his arms out. The barman came up and took hold of Jules by the collar and forced him backwards over the bar. The barman shouted 'Get the police!' The others stopped fighting. The man in the leather coat picked up a glass and raised it and turned to the barman. The barman let go of Jules. The man threw the glass into a corner, where it smashed. Someone screamed.

Jules and the man in the coat pushed their way into the street and ran in different directions. Jules went round a corner crouching, and jumped on a moving bus. He climbed to the top and sat on the front seat.

He changed buses at Marble Arch and walked to his lodgings. There was a portico of crumbling plaster and an open front door. He went to the second floor. His room was narrow with just a bed, wash-stand, chest of drawers, linoleum, and a half-unpacked suitcase. He locked the door and pulled the chest of drawers against it and wedged it with the wash-stand. One of the legs of the wash-stand was twisted and half came off. Jules banged at it. Then he closed the window. He sat on the edge of the bed and shook his head from side to side and rubbed his hands up and down his thighs. He smiled. After a time he leaned back and lit a cigarette. His fingers were shaking, and tobacco shredded out at the ends.

Harry looked at the vertical row of buttons at the side of a front entrance door, each with its card in a slot beside it with a name – FRY, HUSON, GRODOTSKI AND PALMER, and, at the top, LONGLEY. He pressed the top button and leaned towards the grille of a speaker let into the wall. Traffic went past in the street behind. The speaker was chromium-plated with the front of

70

each slot curved downwards. There was a click and an electric scraping sound and Annie's voice saying 'Yes?'

'This is me, Harry.'

The scraping went on. Harry bent closer.

'I'm sorry, I thought you rang the other day.'

'Yes,' Annie said.

'I thought I'd come round to see how you are.'

He was leaning with one hand in his pocket and the other pressed against his thigh. He blinked.

'You're all right?' he said.

'Do you want to come up?' Annie said.

'I think so,' Harry said.

There was a buzz from the front door, which made him jump. It swung open. The scraping noise clicked off. Harry went into a small hall with a lift and a flight of stairs. He sat on the bottom step. It was of stone with a green carpet fastened at the back with clips. His heart thumped. The door through which he had come was of frosted glass in an iron framework.

He climbed up the stairs and rang another bell. Annie was wearing a green corduroy dress with a black belt. She said 'Come in.' Harry said 'Thank you.'

There were rooms slotted into one another like a Chinese puzzle. The doors had chromium handles high up. The walls were cream.

'Do sit down,' Annie said.

'I only wanted to see you, I won't stay a minute.'

'You thought I mightn't be well?'

'Yes.'

'Poor darling!' Annie said.

Harry sat in a chair with the arms and the back fitting

into each other in planes. He said 'What have you been doing?'

'Working very hard, there's such a demand!'

'On the *Post*?'

'And magazines, you know.'

'I'm so glad.' He waited. There was an air-conditioner in the window, switched off. The window was closed. He said 'Why did you ring me?'

'It's a little difficult,' Annie said. 'Would you like a drink?'

Harry said 'Have you got tomato juice?'

While she poured it she said 'So good for you, like Ovaltine.' She sat down opposite him. She said 'You don't mind what I say, do you?'

'No,' Harry said.

'What you are doing is so unimportant, you know?'

Harry said 'Is that what you wanted to tell me?'

'Please don't be angry,' Annie said. 'I am trying to help.

She opened the palms of her hands on her lap. She held her head on one side. 'There's a great deal known about this now. It's no good trying to help people like that.'

'Like what?' Harry said.

'You see – the kind of things you're doing may make you feel good – '

'Oh!' Harry said.

Annie smiled at her hands.

'I'm sorry, go on.'

'You see, you are angry.'

'I'm not,' Harry said.

72

'It may make you feel good, but it won't help anyone else. You can only hurt people like that. It really is important to help oneself first.'

'All right,' Harry said.

'The Help Thy Neighbour Service!' Annie said. 'It sounds like the cleaners!'

'I've heard that one,' Harry said.

'You're intelligent really,' Annie said. She looked straight at him. 'I can talk like this can't I?'

'Yes,' Harry said. His heart was thumping.

Annie clasped her hands carefully. 'Do you know your motives?'

'No one ever knows their motives.'

'There's a great deal of anger in you,' Annie said. 'You want to hide it. Then you're ashamed and want to make up for it.' She moved a ring up and down on her finger. Harry sat still with his arms along the sides of the chair.

'You want to be loved,' Annie said. 'You have a terrible need for it, but it's wrong to project your need on to other people. You don't love them, you only want something from them. You must see what you're doing. You're really still searching – ' She swallowed.

'For what?' Harry said.

'I am trying to help,' Annie said. She had tears in her eyes.

'Yes,' Harry said.

'A mother,' Annie said.

'Oh Lord!' Harry said.

'You won't face it,' Annie said. 'You run away!'

'How do you know what I do?' Harry said.

73

'You won't do the vital things,' Annie said. 'You cut yourself off – '

'What vital things?' Harry said.

'At the centre,' Annie said. 'Your marriage fails and you leave your wife – '

'I leave my wife?'

'Yes,' Annie said. Her face was white. 'Then you leave me, and evade all responsibility, and take to the Church as of course people do and that gives you comfort – '

'Annie darling – ' Harry said.

'Don't call me darling!' Annie said. She held the top of one finger and pulled at it. She went on 'And that satisfies you. It's so weak! What are you going to do with your life? Everything fails! Your work, poetry. Why don't you go back to your wife, it's her I pity.'

'I can't stand this,' Harry said.

'And now you come to me again, it's so unfair!' She put a hand in front of her face.

'I'm going,' Harry said. He stood up.

'You're running away!' Annie said.

Harry had moved to the door and he stopped on one leg and put his hand in his hair. He bent, with his face screwed up. He turned and said 'You know you've got me, don't you?'

Annie was leaning back with her eyes closed.

'You may be right,' Harry said. 'But you shouldn't say those things.' He walked towards her.

'Sit down,' Annie said.

'You don't know what you're doing.' He sat in the armchair.

They seemed to be asleep for a while. A telephone

74

began ringing in the next room. Annie did not move. There was a sound of hammering on the floor below.

When the telephone stopped Annie said 'Another call for help ignored!' She laughed. 'Would you like a drink?'

'Oh, if I'm so weak,' Harry said.

Annie poured a gin and tonic. When she gave it to him she let her finger stroke along the back of his hand. She said 'Have you seen Lydia?'

'Yes,' Harry said.

'Benjy is so sweet, don't you think?' She went to the window and ran her hand over the air-conditioner. 'I must tell you a story, he was going to oppose the homosexuality Bill in the Lords, because he didn't think people really did that, don't you think that's sweet?'

Harry said 'Who told you?'

'Do you mind?' Annie said.

Harry was looking away. He had taken a sip of his drink. The flavour was more scented than he remembered. An impression came to him of a street with small stationers' and grocers' shops and alarm bells ringing.

'Poor darling, are you tired?' Annie said. 'Just stay here quietly for a minute.'

'Then I'll go,' Harry said. In his mind he was running down the street in the sun past stalls of vegetables and bright oranges.

'What are you thinking?' Annie said.

'Nothing,' Harry said. He took another sip.

'How did you know where I was?'

'Someone told me.'

The street Harry was imagining had a bookshop in it with pictures in the window of enormous nudes. Beside

75

it was a gramophone-shop playing jazz music. The sound drifted over the street.

'Did you really think I was trying to get you back?' Annie said.

'No, everything's more complicated,' Harry said.

'You were jolly slow in coming if I was!' Annie said. She laughed.

Harry finished his drink. He stood up.

'Do you remember – ' Annie began.

'Yes.'

'That day on the downs – you knew I was going to say that?'

'Yes,' Harry said.

'You're going?'

She sat with her legs underneath her and her head in profile. Harry went to the door past her, and put his fingers on her head. He said 'Running away?' In his mind he was skipping towards the swing doors of the pub. Standing there was a girl with amber-coloured hair. The street was beautiful.

2

Jenny woke in the large double bed of the room with pale and rather feminine-looking furniture. She was alone. Sitting up with her hair falling forwards so that in profile only her mouth and the end of her nose were visible, she listened. She bent to the floor and felt for her clothes. On the bedside table there was a pencilled note which said *Gone out, back at 10, getting breakfast.*

The light from the curtained windows mixed with the pink glow of an electric fire. Jenny climbed out of bed pulling a sheet and wrapping it round her. She picked up her handbag and went on to the landing. It was cold. There was an open door which led into a smaller bedroom which had a cactus and a model of the Taj Mahal on the window-sill. Beyond it was the bathroom.

She leaned toward a mirror above a shelf smeared with the white rings of a tooth-mug. Turning her head, she lifted with one finger the hair that hung over her face and stretched an eye wide. Above and below it her lids were darkened like soot. She brushed a finger along the lower lid and smoothed the line that went upwards from the corner. She took a hand-mirror from her bag and looked at herself in profile. There was her mouth and the end of her nose visible.

She went into the smaller bedroom holding her arms crossed and her shoulders hunched. She looked at the titles of books in a bookcase. There were *The Cricket Match*, *The Guinness Book of Records*, and *Electricity For You*. She bent to the lower shelves, clasping her sheet. She shivered. She went round the room screwing up her eyes but not touching anything.

When she was back in bed she opened the cupboard beneath the bedside table. Inside there were the four telephone directories, an old copy of *The Tatler*, and a notebook in stiff covers. Jenny took the notebook and opened it at the first page. There was a heading in spidery handwriting *Manifestations of Divine Love*.

Jenny laid the notebook aside and opened *The Tatler*. On an inside page was a large portrait of a woman with a beautiful oval face and long fair hair. The caption said *Mrs Harry Gates, daughter of General and Mrs Winston Adams, of New York*.

Jenny sat up and turned the page to catch the light. Then she picked up the notebook. She lay on her side with one arm propping up her head. She read

Manifestations of Divine Love

The sky touched the earth with its feet and hands
Its body the meridian. Daily
The sun scratched it like a dog's ribs
Arching and stretching its blue bones
Shimmering. Below on the ground

The cactus grew: the long-stemmed grass
Star-pointed and bell-knived
A fakir-bed for summer.

An island. Dropped into the sea
Land: a fin of rock
For air to sharpen on: fire
Struck by flint from it: iron
In the bruised rock-veins
The glint and power
Of the angry sun.

On one side of the island was the deep
Where waves came slowly, mountains moving
Blue-black across the world, blowing
Like whales, trapping the air
In rocks and caves, spouting
Stale as a sodden body bursting
The heave of the sea. And on the other
The coral, beauty's cemetery
Each polyp, shell, a skeleton
Of pink-white tombs; each grain
A universe; the crystal sand
Exact and patterned in the mind of God
But dead; the shallows
Shaking among skulls of crabs
And starfish bones in galaxies.

On to this rock, my love, we came
Not chained by gods but free
As orphans are, from the past
And what would nourish us.

You lay upon the rock midway
Between the deep sea sucking
And the silver sand (my love),
And the dust flew around you
The wheat of insects and the seeds
Of humming-birds; the heat
Making a pool upon your throat deep
As a well; the sweat
From the wet sun; your body
White as the moon.
From the sea (on one side) came the leap
Of the wind in the dark, the hiss
Heaving, the torn
Membrane of oblivion. From the other
The crab crawling into the mouth, the throat
Of coral; to make its tomb there
Scratching its chosen skeleton
Safe from the sea.
I climbed the high hill, the island spine,
The knife to cut us with. Through thorns
And cactus and the steel grass
I saw no resting place: only the two truths
Beneath us, with us; the terror of the ocean
Which was life, and the coral death;
And in between them man, and you,
(My love) and me walking
Below the domed sky
A god or a gorilla.
(Along this violet line,
Time's covenant, you walk or fall.)
And seeing now no hope

No good nor evil, nothing
But the madman or the power
No love; I screamed
As a train will scream
As it sees the cut tracks
The blown bridge
Before the nightmare. Or rather
(Because of you, my love)
The body on the line
And the wheels roaring
And the metal heat unstoppable.

The rock where you lay had been a fort
Where generals in plumes once stood
And beat tattoos on drums
And blew thin bugles. Now
On a ledge of stone
A cannon by you
I stood with my monkey's arms
And dreamed of death: no burden
On the tightrope world, no body
On the rails' guillotine (the rails
Singing Give up, Give up, Man, Man
Is free). And you, my love,
Among the banners and trumpets
Of old love's splendour
Alive to me.

Your body white
Water and stone
Secretly
The pool at your throat

The heart's well
Bottomless
Seeing my face
Narcissus
Mad
Hanging
And no other way
Though endless
Because the plummet
Murdered me.

Jenny heard a door opening. She put the notebook down.
There were footsteps. She lay and put her hands behind
her head. Harry came in. He saw the notebook open on
the bed. Jenny said 'I've been so lonely!' 'You do look
beautiful,' Harry said. 'Hoo-ray!' Jenny said. She held
her arms out.

Lord Sykes and the young man with fair hair sat in the
front seat of the Rolls Royce in a traffic jam in south-
east London. The line of cars moved at the front and
then gathered itself like a worm. The young man said
'What kind of fruit?'

'Melon,' Lord Sykes said.

'What composer?'

'Monteverdi.'

'Another.'

'Mahler.'

'You are clever,' the young man said. He leaned out
of the window. 'All these cars, what are they doing?'

'I read somewhere cars are a sex symbol,' Lord Sykes said. 'When you buy one, you're looking for a mistress.'

'Everything's a sex symbol,' the young man said. 'What Belgian dramatist?'

'Maeterlinck.'

'What character in Proust?'

'I don't know.'

'Morel. Are you alive or dead?'

'Dead,' Lord Sykes said.

'This is so boring,' the young man said. 'Who's Lydia got staying?'

'Leo Johnson I think.'

'Oh how amusing!' the young man said. 'Does Lydia go to him?'

'He's rather her archetype.'

'I once met him with Melissa Gates,' the young man said. 'What's happened to Melissa?'

'Hopped it,' Lord Sykes said. He hooted on the horn.

'Who with?'

'I don't know. I thought it was Harry with that Annie Longley.'

'I rather adored Melissa,' the young man said.

Lord Sykes sat with his hands on top of the steering wheel, a soft green hat on his head. He said 'I never understood Melissa. Always so serious, worrying about things. Half-American, I suppose.'

'Was it Melissa who tried to kill herself?'

'Harry, I thought.'

'Both probably. I remember a weekend when they were having one of their rows, I was in the next room, there were terrible groans.'

'What were they up to?'

'I never asked.'

'You shouldn't marry someone you can't handle,' Lord Sykes said.

The young man looked at him. The corners of his blue eyes wrinkled.

'Something very tough about Melissa,' Lord Sykes said. 'Very beautiful of course.'

'You make her sound quite frightening,' the young man said.

Lord Sykes felt for a cigarette and fitted it into his holder. The air shimmered above the bonnet of the Rolls Royce. He said 'You sometimes come across those people. Seem to be on a different sort of plane. My mother was like that.' He pulled a cigarette-lighter from the dashboard, and puffed. The young man's smile became set, showing his large white teeth.

'Bit of a gorgon,' Lord Sykes said. 'Saw right through you.' He slanted the holder up in his teeth. 'Where were we in the game?'

'You're a woman and you're dead, aren't you?'

'Yes.'

'Madame de Maintenon.'

'You're not allowed a direct question.'

'Oh no. What animal?' the young man said.

Jules poked his head out of the door of his room and looked at a man sitting cross-legged inside a cupboard on the landing. The cupboard was large and double-doored, without shelves or partitions. The doors were open, showing some clothes hanging over a rail and underneath, in front of the seated man, some pots and pans and a primus stove. The man wore black trousers and sweater and had a blue woollen skiing cap on his head. He was cooking bacon.

'Feeding the inner atman, eh?' Jules said.

'I know what you want, Cavendish,' the man said. He had a long mournful face and was chewing inside his closed mouth.

'Nah,' Jules said. He dragged a chair from his bedroom and sat down and watched. He said 'I've got a new idea, listen?'

'Listen,' the man in the cupboard said.

'When a solid body approaches the speed of light, its mass increases, right?'

'Right,' the man said.

'If it reaches the speed of light, its mass is infinite. Therefore there's no speed of light. Light's instantaneous. When you measure it, you're measuring distance.'

The man in the cupboard picked up a bit of bacon from the frying-pan and dropped it, thrashing his fingers about.

'You mean a criticism of measurement,' he said.

Jules leaned forward intently. 'People go off on a ten-year rocket trip, see? They come back to earth in ten years' earth time, five years their time. Well, what's the difference?'

'They're in a different bloody place I suppose,' the man said.

'No.'

'A different bloody shape then for God's sake,' the man said.

'No.'

'Well they can't be stretched half-way round the bloody orbit.' The man flicked up a piece of bacon in his fingers and caught it in his mouth and chewed steadily.

'All right, measurement's out,' Jules said. 'What's left?'

'Samadhi I suppose,' the man in the cupboard said.

'Nah!' Jules said. He groaned.

There was the sound of a front door opening. The man in the cupboard unscrewed the pressure of the primus stove and it wheezed gently. He dragged a jacket from the rail and covered the frying-pan and pots with it. A smartly dressed Indian came up the stairs. He carried a small suitcase. He said 'Mr Cartwright, I have asked you a hundred times not to fry in that cupboard.'

'I pay my rent man,' the man in the cupboard said.

'It smells disgusting. What do you think my other tenants say?'

'What do you say, Cavendish?' the man in the cupboard said.

'I think there's such a disgusting smell here anyway,' Jules said slowly; 'that when Cartwright gets up in the morning, it's like a breath of roses.'

'Please have your money ready when I come down,' the Indian said.

He disappeared up the stairs. The man in the cupboard squatted, put all his things into a rucksack, including the primus stove, still hot, which made him thrash his fingers about; and the frying-pan, still greasy, in the folds of a blue pin-stripe jacket; then he heaved the rucksack on to his back and went off down the stairs in bare feet. Jules closed the cupboard doors behind him.

When the Indian came back he put his suitcase down and opened a notebook and Jules gave him thirty shillings. 'Still two pounds owing last week,' the Indian said. 'Yes,' Jules said. 'And Mr Cartwright?' the Indian said. 'Mr Cartright?' Jules said. The Indian opened the cupboard. 'Oh I see, there is no Mr Cartwright.' 'Doesn't look like it,' Jules said. 'Where is he?' the Indian said.

'I'll tell you,' Jules said. He leaned forward and spoke mysteriously. 'He was sitting here, cross-legged, not much farther than I am from you. And he had a little rope, and he threw it into the air, and he climbed up it, and he disappeared, pffft!' He waved an arm.

'Oh I see,' the Indian said. He did up his suitcase. 'That cupboard has caused me nothing but trouble, I will have it closed.' 'Someone might want to hang their clothes in it,' Jules said. 'What would any of you people want with clothes?' the Indian said. He started off down the stairs. 'We can't all be civilized!' Jules shouted after him. 'I'll get a bit of board and board it up!' the Indian shouted. 'That'll be a nice bit of firewood!' Jules shouted.

The front door banged. Jules went to his room and dressed in an old grey suit and a dark blue shirt buttoned at the neck with no tie. He brushed his hair into a fringe. He went out on the landing and stopped, sniffing. He opened the cupboard and peered in. He picked up a piece of bacon off the floor and flicked it into his mouth, chewing.

'But what happened with you and Annie?' Jenny said. She lay in the bedroom where the curtains were still drawn and shadows from outside moved as if in an aquarium.

'Annie!' Harry said. He lay on his back with his hands folded across his chest. 'Annie and I never touched earth, we comforted one another.'

'Did you love her?'

'Oh yes,' Harry said.

'Why did it stop?'

'Why does it stop?' Harry said. He made a noise like a groan. 'You know too much.'

'Do you live here alone?' Jenny said.

'My son's away at school,' Harry said. His smile became set, showing his teeth. 'Annie and I –' he began.

'But d'you work at that place?' Jenny said.

'Where you rang up?'

'Yes, what do you do?'

'I do some work with the probation office, too, there was a boy staying here the other day.'

'I do think it's good of you,' Jenny said.

'Annie and I met when I was doing a welfare course at London University,' Harry said. 'She was doing a survey or something. We used to go to the British Museum –' He waited. 'We were very ordinary.'

'Did she know Maurice?' Jenny said.

'Then we – you know –' Harry screwed up his face

' – we used to go to the pub – then I was with her one day when someone at home got ill – ' He stopped.

'Who?' Jenny said.

'It doesn't help if you say it was a dream.'

'What was Maurice doing?' Jenny said.

'I've never talked about it to anyone before,' Harry said.

'Baby, you talk about it.'

'You are good to me,' Harry said.

'Oh I'm not!' Jenny said. She put down a coffee cup and leaned towards him.

Harry said, 'Let's go away somewhere, let's go to Japan.'

'People are always arranging flowers in Japan.'

'You have such information.'

'I get it from women's magazines.'

Harry said 'Let's stay in bed all day.'

'I was reading your poem,' Jenny said. 'I like it. You did write it, didn't you?'

'Oh yes,' Harry said. He became suddenly animated. He sat up and opened the notebook. 'Look at it – ' He turned the pages. 'Crazy stuff!' He started reading. He pulled at his lower lip.

'Where was it?' Jenny said.

Harry said 'An island. In the Caribbean.'

'Did you go there?'

'Yes,' Harry said. 'Listen – "below the domed sky a god or a gorilla". There's evil, you're frightened.' He turned over some pages. 'But then if you face it, it goes.' He frowned. 'No that's not true.'

'What happened?' Jenny said.

'I once tried to shoot myself,' Harry said. 'Oh – long after the island.'

Jenny looked at him.

'A bit of plaster fell from the ceiling,' Harry said. He threw the notebook away. 'Oh what nonsense! I only pretended.'

'I think it's rather like some of Jerril's poems,' Jenny said.

'I think I'm like Jerril,' Harry said: 'don't you?'

'Not a bit,' Jenny said.

'Jerril's a monster.'

'Was your poem about Annie?'

'Oh no no no no,' Harry almost sang. 'The real thing, the come-uppance, my wife Melissa.

Jerril knelt with the top half of his body over a sheet of plate glass which lay on the floor in a steel frame. At the back of it was what looked like adhesive paper of different colours. Jerril felt the surface with his fingers. The room in which he knelt was the L-shaped drawing-room on the first floor of a London house, now turned into a studio with a wooden floor littered with tools, a carpenter's bench, two easels, wood-shavings, large pots of paint and strips of metal. Jerril held a hammer and small iron punch in his hand. He tapped against the glass and it splintered, becoming opaque, with tiny white lines radiating outwards like stars. The surface of the glass stayed flat, and Jerril pressed on it. There appeared from underneath the colour, or dye, from the paper at the back which had a solution on it; and it spread in reds and oranges and greens in the miniscule cracks like veins. By his taps on the hammer Jerril altered the size and shape of the stars, and by sliding his hand over the surface he guided the radiations. The colours appeared just after his hand had passed, so that they seemed to come alive like dry seaweed with water poured over it. Afterwards, he covered the glass with a liquid which made the colours grow closer to the surface. When the solution dried, the effect was of something seen beneath water – a distortion of sand and shells and coral.

Annie came into the room and said 'Do you want them up?' Jerril said nothing. Annie went downstairs. Jerril heard her letting people in at the front door.

There came into the studio first a tall man with spectacles and a black jacket and striped trousers, and then the old man with white hair and a bright red face. The man in striped trousers said 'This is Lord Sidney.' Jerril stood up and said 'How do you do.' He held his shoulders hunched and his head on one side. The old man took his hand and stared at him with his small black eyes like truffles. He held his heavy rubber-tipped walking stick. Jerril went to the far end of the room.

The man in striped trousers began whispering 'This is very fine, he must have been working on it, the colours are good.' The two men stared at the piece of glass on the floor. Jerril sat on a stool. 'The sense of sharpness is very strong,' the man in striped trousers said. The old man moved round the plate of glass, leaning on his stick. He looked at some objects on the carpenter's bench by the window. There were globes of iron that seemed to have holes in them blown from the

91

inside by explosive; pieces of wood axed with chips so that they looked like palm-trees; one oil painting on the wall of a nude with the veins visible like leaves. The man in striped trousers said 'Everything is exploding, opening. Nothing is created.' The old man stared at the nude. Jerril watched them.

'Growth,' the man in striped trousers said. He made a circle with his hands.

'Now that's what I understand,' the old man said.

Jerril walked over and took down the picture of the nude. He carried it to where he had been sitting and leaned it with its face to the wall.

'I came here to buy!' the old man shouted.

'Shall we look at more glass?' the man in striped trousers said.

'Do you sell this stuff?' the old man shouted. He stared at the pane of glass on the floor.

'Mind your walking stick, please,' Jerril said.

The old man shifted his stick slightly so that it poked the glass on the floor.

'Get out' Jerril shouted. He jumped off his stool.

The old man turned his back and began examining the pieces of iron. The holes in them had ragged edges like petals. The man in striped trousers held his hands out towards Jerril. Jerril began opening all the windows.

Annie appeared and stood in the doorway. She said 'Would you be kind and go?'

'I'll come back later,' the man in striped trousers whispered.

Jerril was trying to fan the air out of the windows. He said 'I can't breathe!'

'I've enjoyed my visit very much!' the old man shouted at Annie. He shook hands with her. 'I'm a great admirer of your work Miss Longley! I'm proud to have you on my staff'

Annie went with them downstairs. There was a crash of something heavy above them. When she went back to the studio Jerril was not there. One of the easels was on its side. There was a smell of varnish and spirit gum.

She went up to the second floor and stood on the landing. She said 'Can I come in?' She tried the handle of a door. It was locked.

Through the narrow window half-way up the stairs she saw a line of chimneys and television aerials. There was the branch of a tree with white patches on it, and leaves of surprising green. Annie called – 'I'm next door.' She went into a room which was like a junk shop. There were packing cases and old furniture and one armless statue at an angle against the wall. She brushed the dust off a red velvet chair with tassels, and sat down. In front of her was a glass dome of stuffed birds. The eyes of the birds were buttons on the ends of needles. The telephone was beside her on its three-legged chair propped up by books.

'Oh come in,' Father Patterson said, seeing Jules on the doorstep in his dark grey suit and blue shirt buttoned at the neck; 'just in time for lunch.' 'Sorry, I tried to get 'ere earlier,' Jules said. 'Don't worry,' Father Patterson said. ''Ad a bit of trouble with me landlord,' Jules said.

They went through a hall with a row of black coats on hooks and a shelf of pigeon-holes. 'I don't even know

your name,' Father Patterson said. 'Jules Cavendish.'
'Jules?' Father Patterson said, pronouncing it as in
French. 'Jules,' Jules said, pronouncing it like Jewels.
'Come along,' Father Patterson said.

There was a small bare dining-room with six monks
standing looking in different directions like officers on
the bridge of a ship. They wore black cassocks and
leather belts with small crucifixes hanging from them.
Father Patterson showed Jules to a chair on his right at
the head of the table. The monks stood behind their
chairs while Father Patterson said grace. He introduced
Jules to them. The monk on the other side of Jules was
an old man with a round cheerful face. He said, 'Do you
live in town, Mr Cavendish?'

'Paddington,' Jules said.

'Is that an interesting part of London?'

'Ve – ry.' Jules spoke in his drawl.

'But not architecturally distinguished, I believe.'

Jules suddenly found food passed to him from all
sides – cold meat, baked potatoes, salad, bread, pickles,
mustard, and a cucumber. He said 'More the people.
Bunch of weirdies.'

'Please help yourself, Mr Cavendish,' the old monk
said. Jules had got hold of the cucumber and was slicing
it away from him like sharpening a pencil. 'Weirdies is
a word I haven't come across before,' the old monk said.

'Lots of Indians,' Jules said: 'Landlords.'

'I trust they treat you well?'

'Charge you for sleeping in a cupboard.'

'That must be unusual,' the old monk said.

'Oh there are lots of rackets.' Jules said. He banged at

the bottom of a bottle of salad-dressing and a drip came out. 'Allow me,' the old monk said. He took the bottle and waved it round his ear: then poured it on to Jules's plate. 'There is a technique. I'm sorry – rackets?'

'The Cypriots run most of the girls,' Jules said.

The old monk said 'That is very interesting.'

Jules sighed. 'Aye, you see a thing or two!'

The old monk turned to the monk on his other side and said 'Mr Cavendish has been telling me about conditions in Paddington.' The other monk said 'I'm never exactly clear how far Paddington goes.'

Jules's plate was taken away and bananas and custard put in front of him. He sat with his hands folded inwards beneath his thighs. He said 'I got in a fight yesterday as a matter of fact. I was lucky to get away.' He began speaking in his mock-cockney. 'I was in a pub, see, 'avin' a beer. Then along comes these three men. Well we knows 'em, see? an' they says somethin' to us. An' there we are.'

'I suppose a certain amount of that is unavoidable,' the old monk said.

The other monks were busy taking plates away and stacking them.

Father Patterson said 'Does your family live in London?'

'Me mother's in 'ospital and me father's dead,' Jules said.

'Any brothers or sisters?'

'No, I've got a grandfather, I work for him.'

'What work is that?' Father Patterson said.

95

'Newspapers,' Jules said. 'My grandfather owns a newspaper.'

Father Patterson brushed some crumbs off the table. He said 'Your mother – will she be coming out of hospital?'

'Oh no – ' Jules said. He seemed to sing. 'No, she won't.'

Father Patterson looked round the table. He said 'Have we finished?' They all stood up. Father Patterson said grace. He said 'Shall we go to my room?'

Lydia sat on a *chaise longue* with her profile silhouetted against a window through which could be seen a tendril of wisteria and beyond it a ploughed field. Dr Johnson frowned in the opposite direction with his fingers in his jacket pockets, his thumbs on the outside pointing forwards. There was the sound of laughter from the next room. Lydia said 'Who is this boy?'

Dr Johnson said 'Do you know his mother, Emma?'

Lydia said 'I've got people this afternoon.'

'You think it's homosexual?' Dr Johnson said.

Lydia closed her eyes. The room was part of a low-beamed cottage with large windows and furniture that seemed cut off at the legs. Lydia said slowly 'Benjy – is – normal.'

Dr Johnson rattled the money in his pocket. He said 'Being normal can be – ' he frowned and moved his lips in and out ' – a defence.'

Lydia leaned over the edge of the *chaise-longue* and looked up out of the corners of her eyes like a little girl. She giggled. 'Are we all perverted?'

The butler came in carrying coffee-cups. He was followed by Lord Sykes and the young man with fair hair. Lord Sykes moved his arms, stretching his neck and shoulders. Lydia poured out coffee. She gave a cup to Dr Johnson. The young man said 'What pretty cups!'

Dr Johnson said softly 'Lydia, what shall I tell Parks this afternoon?'

'Could you be an angel and say there'll be eleven for tea?' Lydia said.

Dr Johnson walked slowly to the door.

Lord Sykes picked up a Sunday newspaper and said 'Benjy bad boy, late for lunch.'

The young man took a coffee-cup and Lydia poured coffee into it. He said 'It was my fault really.'

'Sent upstairs,' Lord Sykes said.

Dr Johnson came back and said softly 'Parks wants to know about dinner.'

'Naughty Benjy!' Lord Sykes said. He folded his paper and patted himself with it on the behind.

Lydia crossed her hands on her lap. She looked out of the window. There was an orchard of fruit-trees in symmetrical rows. White blossom was beginning. The ploughed earth was a golden brown.

Dr Johnson went up to the young man so that he was almost touching him, and said 'How is Emma these days?'

'She's very well!' the young man said. His face lit up.

Lord Sykes opened his paper. There was a headline – *What We Do When We Think*.

Dr Johnson stood in front of the fireplace. The grate had three logs of the same length placed across wrought iron stands. Underneath was a conical pile of ash. The windows of the room were closed. From underneath came a faint roaring sound like that of a ship.

Lord Sykes read *Anne Longley reports on recent researches in the Mind*.

The young man sat on a low stool with his knees up round his chin. He put his arms round his legs and hugged them.

Lydia's face was empty. Her eyes were like a swimming pool that has been drained.

Harry lay in bed with his head propped on his arm and the notebook open beside him. He was alone. From along the passage came the noise of water splashing. He read:

> We climbed the long tower
> Where smoke and the smell of bats
> Had scorched the stone walls
> With worshippers (this sacrifice
> Not of the sun
> But of age and decay and dirt).
> You climbed ahead of me
> The inward channel of my mind
> That other part of me
> I never knew nor wanted to
> But attached to me with a climber's
> Umbilical love. At the top
> Where the black passage opened
> You stopped, seeing a landscape
> Of minarets and domes, a town

Old as an anthill, and beyond it
The river and palm-trees and the sand.
There was a space within the parapet
Where once some armament had stood
With iron buttressed at the sides
And at the centre, flat, a hole
Falling to the courtyard far below
And infinite as dying. You crossed this gap
How, with no head for miracles,
I do not know: then leaned
On the gold wall, looking
At the shape, the light
Of the lovely landscape. And I
Who live more in myself
Like a book with yellow pages
When I asked – May I
Have your hand, my love – You turned
As one will undress quickly
To the necessities of love; and there
With your care, your gentle rectitude
Saw me half-way over, and then left me
Knowing again the somnolence of things
Turning and tumbling downwards as a dream.

Harry lowered his forehead until it rested on the book.
He drew his knees up so that he was half kneeling. He
put his arms at the back of his head and with the edge
of one hand hit against his neck. He made a sneezing
noise.

Jenny came in from the bathroom. She was wrapped

in a yellow towel. Harry looked up. He said 'You're like someone in a foreign film.'

'That is for ever England,' Jenny said. She crossed a fist against her shoulder and stood on one leg.

Harry climbed off the bed. He took hold of her and began to dance. He said 'Qu'est-ce que tu fais ce soir?'

'Je suis facile chéri,' Jenny said.

'Je ne te laisserai jamais,' Harry said. 'Je vais avec toi jusqu'aux bords de la terre.' They circulated round the room doing a foxtrot.

'Jusqu'au pays d'où on ne reviendra pas,' Jenny said. She threw her head back.

'Oh do you know that?' Harry said.

'Let's go somewhere where people will clap us!' Jenny said.

'For your sweet face and my new clothes,' Harry said.

'Oh, in the fall of '16!' Jenny said. 'Baby!'

'You see,' Jules said, rubbing his hands along his thighs, 'man's got to surpass himself – think more, feel more. But he's got to go with history.'

Father Patterson sat on his bed with his head against the wall. Jules was opposite him on the one chair of the bare room which contained just bed, table, chest of drawers, chair, wash-stand and crucifix. Father Patterson said 'Where's history going?'

'There's an energy,' Jules said. 'People don't know. They move blindly, without will. You have to feel it.'

'How?' Father Patterson said.

'That's difficult,' Jules said. He rocked backwards and

forwards. 'Sensitivity. Like an instrument.' He held his hand vertical and turned it as if to the wind. 'Circling.' He frowned. 'Not like the beatniks, they're slaves. But choice, decision.' At each word he twisted his hand as if screwing something up.

'You've only got one life,' Father Patterson said.

'Oh I know,' Jules said. 'I don't think I'm doing it!' He opened his eyes wide and pursed his lips.

'You work on a newspaper?' Father Patterson said.

'Administration.'

'D'you like it?'

'Oh, it's rotten!' Jules said. 'Some decent men, but so stupid!'

'What work would you like?' Father Patterson said. He sat bolt upright.

'I've thought of that,' Jules said. He shrugged.

'Anyone can have theories,' Father Patterson said. 'You've got to test them against yourself.'

'Yourself!' Jules said. He twisted his face up.

'How much do you see of those people you were with yesterday?'

'One or two friends,' Jules said.

'Do you know why you don't break with them? Because to make a choice, decision, is very difficult.'

'Oh I know,' Jules said. He rocked backwards and forwards as if in pain.

'It costs something.'

'What?'

'In the small things. You've got to live it.' Father Patterson watched him. 'You're intelligent.'

'I don't know – ' Jules said. 'I wonder – ' He put a hand to his head. 'I sometimes feel I'm a bit mad!'

'You'll be all right,' Father Patterson said.

'I don't tell the truth,' Jules said. 'I know I don't.' He gripped his knees.

'Do you pray?' Father Patterson said.

Jules stared at him. 'No.'

'Try it.'

'Oh I don't think – '

'It will come into your head,' Father Patterson said. His face went flat. 'At the important moments, you either do or you don't, anyway. Everyone does. You have a choice.'

'Oh well I mustn't keep you,' Jules said. He half stood up.

'Then things go on again, but differently.' Father Patterson smiled. 'Do you have to go?'

'I think so, yes,' Jules said. He moved toward the door.

'Come round again,' Father Patterson said.

'Yes,' Jules said.

Father Patterson went downstairs with him. Jules went out into the street and began running with his hands in his pockets. He skipped on the far pavement. Father Patterson watched him; then went into the chapel and sat in his stall and folded his hands. Jules ran to a main road and dodged among the traffic. A thump of music floated across the street. Some boys and girls stood in front of a café, leaning in towards each other and laughing. Jules strode past them. There was a record of a boy's voice crying in an echo-chamber. The street was beautiful.

Maurice Bloxham leaned with his hands on the back of a large leather chair that stood in the gutter of a street of small stationers' and grocers' shops. Across the road, watching him, was a man dressed in black sweater and trousers with a blue woollen skiing cap on his head. He carried a haversack, and had bare feet. Maurice called 'Could you give me a hand?'

The man came over. He said 'That's not a bad chair.'

Maurice said 'It goes quite smoothly if you keep the castors straight.' They each took an arm and began pushing it.

'Why d'you want it?' the man with the haversack said.

'To sit on for God's sake,' Maurice said.

'How much did it cost?'

'Two pounds.'

The chair lurched into the curb. 'Watch it!' Maurice shouted. He took hold of the man's arms. 'Keep the pressure forwards. Balanced!' He spread the man's arms out. They went on.

'D'you want to sell it?' the man said.

'I've only just bought it!' Maurice said.

They came to a crossroads, and stopped. The man sat on an arm of the chair and lifted a foot and examined his bare sole. He said 'These pavements are killing me.'

'Why don't you wear shoes?'

The man took off his haversack and sat in the seat of

the chair. He put his feet on the haversack. He said 'I'll give you two pounds ten.'

'How can you give two pounds ten when you haven't got any shoes?'

The man lay back. Maurice stood with his hands on the back of the chair as if it were a bath chair and the man an invalid. The man said 'Where did it come from?'

'A billiards room.'

'What was it doing in a billiards room for God's sake?'

Maurice leaned forward and stared at the man. A few passers-by had stopped to watch. They were opposite a doorway which said *The Golden Egg*.

'It'd be quicker to carry him,' a passer-by said.

'Would you give me a hand?' Maurice said.

'Surely,' the passer-by said. He leaned down and put an arm beneath the man's knees and the other round his shoulders. He said, 'Easy.'

The passer-by lifted the man. The man clung to him. The passer-by said 'What happened?' The man began laughing a high-pitched laugh with his mouth closed. 'How did you get hurt?' the passer-by said.

'I'm not hurt,' the man said.

The passer-by put him back in the chair. He said 'Is this a joke?'

'Oh leave him alone!' Maurice said.

'Good heavens!' the passer-by said. He went away.

'What size shoes do you take?' Maurice said.

'Twelves.'

'You can't take twelves!' Maurice said.

'You could sleep in this chair,' the man said.

'It's getting dark,' Maurice said.

'Shall I give you a hand?' the man said. They began pushing again.

Annie was in the room like a junk-shop with packing-cases and old furniture. There was the sound of traffic below. Street lights went on in a soft blaze.

Annie lay with her eyes closed. She was walking along a country road in the sun. There was a hedge of hawthorn and the long green sweep of a down. She skipped. Harry was on the other side of the road. He was like a giraffe, moving. The light between them came alive. The earth sloped downwards, swaying.

There was a line running round the world between them. They were at opposite ends of a pole carried by a tightrope-walker who was on this line. They faced forwards to the dark sky but were joined inwards by the pole. They moved in the air as the tightrope-walker moved but it was they who were balancing him. He was a third person between them who moved them but whom, by balancing him, they kept alive.

The sun and the curve of the down was beautiful. She began coming across the road towards him. He stayed where he was.

The pole tilted. The person carrying the pole went down on one knee. She stopped. Harry was somewhere below her. He said 'You must go back.' She said 'Why?' Below them was the darkness and the crowd breathing. There was a spotlight on them. 'Look!' Harry said. The tightrope-walker was hunched against the sky. The pole was resting at right angles to the world. 'I can't,' she said.

She stretched herself out on the pole. It was hard, like a stake. There was an ache inside her. Harry watched her. The world slid downwards. They were in a bedroom with the curtains drawn and a pink glow from an electric fire. Harry was below her. She touched him. They were holding on to each other while the room whirled. They tumbled, weightless. Then the telephone rang.

Annie opened her eyes. She was in the room like a junk shop with packing-cases and old furniture. The telephone was beside her on the three-legged chair propped up by books. She put a hand to it. It was not ringing. She held her hand out, listening.

The house was quiet. Traffic went past in the street below. She tried to remember. Harry was disappearing like someone falling.

She stood up and went on to the landing and listened outside the door of the room that had been locked. She said 'Let me in, I can help you.' The sky outside was dark with a moon at the back of the chimneys and television aerials. She pushed against the door and it opened. Jerril was lying on a bed. She sat beside him. He put his head on her lap. She held him.

Harry had stretched out an arm to the telephone. She had said 'Don't answer it.' He had said 'Who shall I pretend I am?' He had picked it up and listened. He had put his head down and hit the back of his neck with his hand. He had said 'I'll come.' He had already begun to move away from her. 'Who was it?' she had said. 'Someone is ill.' 'Who?' 'Melissa,' he had said.

Lord Sykes stood outside the country cottage on a small

lawn. Through the lighted windows he could see a party in progress. People seemed unnaturally tall owing to the low ceiling and the level of the window. Their heads were squashed and their middles elongated as if on a television screen out of alignment. Lydia was talking to the young man with fair hair. She held her hand on her heart and stretched her eyes at him.

Lord Sykes held a glass of whisky in front of him at the level of his waist. His black shadow cast by the moon was hunched like a dwarf. He set off across the lawn away from the house, stepping over a flower-bed. Beyond it was a barbed-wire fence and a line of trees. He put a leg over the fence, balancing his whisky. He pushed the wire down underneath him. He lurched over. He emerged through the line of trees.

There was a golf course with a flag sticking up on the raised platform of a green and beyond it a bunker. Lord Sykes stood on the green and gazed back down the fairway. A line of trees went each side into the distance. The moon made the grass silver.

He heard someone call from the garden. He crouched, and still holding his whisky stepped down into the bunker. He slid on the soft sand. It was wet. He kept his head down. Dr Johnson's voice, just above him, said 'Hullo there.'

'Hullo 'ullo 'ullo,' Lord Sykes said. He straightened himself. His head came to the top of the bunker. Dr Johnson was standing on the green. Lord Sykes took a sip of whisky.

'I was sent to find you,' Dr Johnson said.

'How's the party?' Lord Sykes said.

'What course is this?'

'The Royal Cliffdown.'

Dr Johnson rattled the money in his pocket. He stood gazing down the fairway. He was holding a glass at the level of his waist.

'What hole?'

'The thirteenth.'

Lord Sykes glanced at Dr Johnson's shoes, just in front of his face. They were made of interwoven strips of leather, like basket-work.

'How do you find Lydia?' Lord Sykes said.

'I think she's all right,' Dr Johnson said.

'She has these migraines,' Lord Sykes said. 'What's the treatment?'

'There are sedatives,' Dr Johnson said. He raised himself on his toes.

'Our way of life's pretty hectic.'

'Suppositories,' Dr Johnson said.

'How did you get over the fence, I nearly got caught, what?'

There was another call from the garden. A cloud went over the moon and shadows rushed across the trees and sea of grass.

'D'you do this electrical treatment?' Lord Sykes said.

'You mean – ?'

'Depression,' Lord Sykes said. He drew his chin so far in that his neck became wrinkled.

'Yes,' Dr Johnson said. He suddenly crouched on the platform of the green. Lord Sykes lowered his whisky. A voice said 'I'm stuck!'

'Peter!' Lord Sykes said. He began climbing out of the bunker.

'Where are you?' the young man with fair hair said. 'This fence!'

Lord Sykes and Dr Johnson approached him. He had one leg over the fence and was pushing the wire down underneath him. Lord Sykes said 'Lift your leg up!'

'I can't.'

'Hold on to my shoulder.'

'I want to go the *other* way.'

'There must be another way on to this golf course.' Dr Johnson said.

The young man hopped over the fence hanging on to Lord Sykes's shoulder. He said 'It's like a camp!'

'How's the party?' Lord Sykes said.

'All right I think. What course is this?'

'The Royal Cliffdown.'

They climbed up on to a tee platform and faced in different directions, like officers on the bridge of a ship. They looked at the grass and the dark trees. 'It's beautiful!' the young man said.

Within the bar of the pub with photographs of boxers on the walls Jenny and Harry sat at a round table with glasses in front of them while the noise moved like an orchestra playing. There were elbows raised like violins and the pursed mouths of woodwinds and a clash of laughter like cymbals. Harry said 'The first time I saw you I wrote a poem about you.' 'To have a poem written about you is like being given music if you're a song,' Jenny said. She bent over the polished table and drew a finger along it. A man swayed with his arms raised. Jenny's eyes were greyish-green.

When he had come here the day before, Harry remembered, she had been sitting where she was now (he always came back like a dog to bones, Harry thought) the line of her hair past her face and her almost invisible lipstick. He had said 'It was kind of you to ring.' 'Did you find Annie?' she had said. Her voice was like a breath making glass misty. 'I wondered if you'd be here,' he had said. 'I wondered,' she had said.

Jenny looked up from the table that was streaked with beer and said 'Are you a Christian, Harry?'

'Yes,' he said.

'Do you go to church and that sort of thing?'

'That sort of thing,' he said. 'I try to.'

There had been a line between them and a curve around the world. The faces of people had been a dark crowd below. There had been a spotlight and the music of silver and brass. He had drunk wine. There had been the smell of powder and the touch of white clothes and he had heard the crowd roaring. Miles above the earth they had turned, bowing. But you can't control the magic, Harry thought: why?

'I love being with you,' Jenny said: 'you make me feel safe.'

They had gone out (last night, the night when he had run through the street with alarm bells ringing) through the swing doors with the brass plate and scratches on it and into the street, the beautiful street, with shops like caves; and he had taken her by the arm, running – she in her grey dress and hair like green gold – the virgin mother, the obedient child – and he the magician. They had come to a road (it was Saturday night) where there were the offices of film companies – windows with small square pictures of the fantasies of the world – and Jenny had sung (how small the world was) 'Baby!' and he had danced, tipping a hat over one eye, swinging between the gutter and the dustbins: 'I can't give you anything but – '

'I cheat,' Jenny said. 'We all cheat. But I don't make demands for things.' She looked at him. She moved a finger on the table streaked with beer. 'I sometimes feel I have no rights.'

They had had dinner across a table with a white cloth and flowers. Her grey dress had been like bark off the skin of a tree. There had been a spirit imprisoned in the tree which was himself. When you made love, you made love to yourself. You walked in a magic wood through fronds of branches. The wood was haunted. Jenny had been waiting for Jerril or for Maurice; he himself had known Annie who knew Jerril or Maurice. You cleared the way with your arms. The princess slept on a dais with her mouth raised. The water washed over it. It was like a sea anemone, or polyp. You were sucked in. You grew.

'When I'm with other people,' Jenny said, 'life's a joke. We never talk to each other. When you say nice things, I don't know whether to believe them.'

They had left the restaurant and gone home (climbing the steps of the throne with the spotlight on them) and he had thought – Like children. They had been in a haystack with their knees up. They had been under water like a submarine. You held it, you touched life. He had climbed on the wet stones, splashing. The trees rushed upwards. You were no longer the beast. The princess came alive.

'I feel I'm like a child,' Jenny had said.

'When I was a child,' Jenny said (pushing her finger along the table, making a circle of streaked beer), 'my father used to get through to my mother by spiritualism. He did automatic writing, and I'd sit with him in the dark. We held hands and each had a hand on the writing-board. We got a message from my mother saying she was close to us.' Jenny laughed.

'I thought the message meant she was next door, so I went to see her. On the way to school there was a house with railings round it that was the lunatic asylum. There was a sort of lodge with a drive going past it. There was a woman just inside doing something to the lawn. When she saw me she lifted her clothes up. I thought she was my mother.'

'How old were you?' Harry said.

'Eight.'

'Did you live alone with your father?'

'Yes. This woman – ' Jenny stopped.

'Where do you live now?' Harry said.

Jenny looked towards the door of the pub. A man dressed in black had come in. He wore a blue woollen skiing cap on his head. 'I left home,' Jenny said.

'You can always stay with me,' Harry said.

Jenny said nothing.

'I mean as you like,' Harry said. He shook his head. 'Any way you like.'

The swing door opened again and the back of a large armchair appeared. The man with the skiing hat was trying to steer it through. He had bare feet. Beyond him, in the street, was a policeman.

Harry said, 'I mean, we needn't always make love.' He put his hand on Jenny's.

Maurice Bloxham's voice shouted 'If I can't leave it here what can I do?'

The barman came from behind the bar. The man with bare feet lifted a leg and hopped with his face screwed up. Maurice began climbing over the chair. The policeman pointed. Maurice shouted to the barman 'I'll pay you!' He pulled on the chair and it came through the door with a rush. The man with bare feet sat on it.

Jenny was watching Maurice. Her face was like an animal on a scent. She said 'Where have you been?'

The barman began pushing the chair with the man with bare feet in it. Maurice sat down by Jenny. He said 'I've been looking for you!'

'You do spend your time,' Jenny said.

'Everywhere,' Maurice said. He moved his head from side to side like a bull.

'Under Annie Longley's bed?' Jenny said.

'I haven't seen Annie!' Maurice said. 'I've been arrested!'

'The only thing arrested is your development.'

'In Whitehall, after the meeting. I spent the night at Cannon Street.'

'Les soirs illuminés par charbon,' Jenny said.

Yesterday, Harry remembered, she had said – Did you

113

see Maurice with Annie? Today, going out – Let's go to
the pub, don't you think?'

The man with bare feet had been pushed in his chair
towards their table. He said 'Have you got any pills?'

'No,' Harry said.

'The ones I like are the little tubular yellow ones.'

'Had a good day, Harry?' Maurice shouted.

'Yes,' Harry said.

'Richard back from school?'

'Next week,' Harry said.

'They make everything go in squares,' the man in the
chair said. 'I don't like the little brown round ones.'

'What do they do?'

'Monsters,' the man said.

Jenny was dressed in her grey woollen dress. It had a
skirt with pleats all round. It was rucked at the back.
Her knees were smooth. She had thin fingers with
brown wrinkles at the edges. She rested her chin on one
wrist. She was listening to Maurice, smiling. There was
a mole on her cheekbone. Her lips were precisely delin-
eated. Her eyebrows had gold in them.

Harry thought – You look forward and back, never to
what you are. Within this triangle love breathes; like a
tightrope-walker with his back bent. There had been
a triangle last night between the bed and the sheet and
Jenny's breast. Jenny had walked on tiptoe, naked. You
balanced, apart. Yet once, you met.

Maurice said to Jenny 'You look like an alsatian with
a deaf-aid.'

Jenny said 'Maurice is so fond of animals.'

Harry finished his glass of gin and tonic. He said 'Maurice, what are you drinking?'

They went into the street (the street they always returned to like dogs), he, Maurice, Jenny, the man with bare feet, and their chair prophetic as a piece of primitive sculpture; pushing it up the pavement like a throne on which the Pharaohs might have sat – the kings of Mycenae and Crete with their mad smiles and straight-backed elbows. Jenny kept close to Maurice as they went past the fronts of restaurants and blank brick walls ('Where shall we go?' Maurice said: 'I know a place,' the man with bare feet said) along the alleyways with dustbins. Jenny walked with her shoulders hunched and her hands crossed in front of her. They were at opposite sides of the pavement, moving. Yet once they had met.

They came to a café with a neon sign of a goose with a large yellow egg. They stared at it. Jenny stood with one ankle turned against the pavement. Harry said 'I've been here before!'

Inside there were red-topped tables with wooden chairs and a counter with sandwiches and soft-drinks cylinders. There was the staircase at the far end with the notice *Members Only*. Harry walked through the tables trailing his fingers. From below there came the thump of a juke-box and a boy's voice crying in an echo chamber. At the bottom of the stairs was a small square hole where you signed your name.

'When you think you've been somewhere before,' Harry said (the man with bare feet was writing; the chair had been left in the café upstairs) 'a cell sometimes has split in your brain and functions separately.' They emerged into a room with square concrete pillars and neon lights. The noise was blaring. 'So how do you know?' Harry shouted. They sat at a table. He faced them – Jenny, Maurice, and the man with bare feet. 'I mean, if you have been or not?' In the middle of the room couples were dancing. There were girls with small brown faces and hair like huge spiders; boys hooped and ringed like Saturn. 'But then you do!' Harry shouted. He clapped his hands. The dancers pirouetted. 'The two cells meet!' He lifted his arms and screwed his face up. He began to dance, clicking his fingers. 'Then everything is beautiful!'

When the music stopped the dancers went back to their tables and sat slouched with their legs apart. There was the smell of powder and cold metal. Their eyes and lips were silver. A boy with orange hair had come and put his arms on the back of the chair of the man with bare feet. The boy was saying 'He's going to board it up. So I told him – that'll be a nice bit of firewood!'

Harry said 'I know your voice.'

They paid no attention to him. The music began again. Maurice and Jenny stood up. There were strings being plucked like an earthquake. The walls went in and out. 'Good night Harry,' Maurice said.

'You're going?' Harry said.

'Let's do something one day, hmm?'

'Partir c'est mourir un peu,' Jenny said. She leaned down and kissed Harry.

'I do know you,' Harry said to the boy. He stood up.

'Who are you?' the boy said.

'Who am I!' Harry said. He ran his hand through

his hair. Jenny and Maurice were disappearing up the staircase. He shouted 'Goodbye!'

'Don't ask me,' the man with bare feet said.

Harry said 'Harry Gates!'

'Harry Gates!' the boy said.

'You do know me?'

'Oh,' the boy said. 'I think so.'

3

The train came into the station with a clank of iron and steam, one piston-shaft of the engine coming to rest opposite Harry (how did it start when both pistons were at extremes? he thought) and the name *Lady Godiva* in brass letters on the boiler. The passengers debouched and turned in column towards the barrier. Harry moved up the platform to where it darkened beneath a bridge and he saw the group of schoolboys in their pale blue caps and grey flannels standing round their luggage and the other parents there before him (how did they know the correct position in the train? he thought) and Richard with his freckled face and blue eyes looking smaller than he had remembered. 'Hullo Richard,' Harry said: 'Oh hullo,' Richard said. 'And how has he been doing this term?' Harry said to the headmaster. He spoke in a breezy voice and rubbed a fist in his other hand. The headmaster bent down to check whom Harry was talking about: 'Cap on straight, tie, we're not always tidy!' 'A family failing!' Harry said with a laugh. The headmaster looked up at Harry from underneath: 'We could do with a little more concentration!' Harry shifted from foot to foot. 'Have a nice holiday,' he said suddenly to the headmaster. The headmaster shook hands wonderingly.

Harry and Richard walked down the platform with Richard carrying an imitation-leather suitcase patched at one corner with sellotape. 'It's an extraordinary thing,' Harry said, 'but I feel like a schoolboy myself.' At the barrier he stopped and searched his pockets. 'Have you got your ticket?' 'Yes,' Richard said. Harry gave up the ticket and went on. 'I don't think I look like a parent, do you?' 'Quite,' Richard said. 'Let's go by underground,' Harry said, 'would you like that?'

'How does the underground work?' Richard said.

'Well,' Harry said. They went down the escalator past the advertisements of women in corsets. There was a new one of a girl lying on the bonnet of a car with her chin in her hand and one high-heeled foot lifted. 'Electric, you know – the trains run every few minutes and there are signals to start and stop them.'

'How many volts?'

'Thousands,' Harry said. He peered over the edge of the platform.

'Can it kill you?'

'Yes.'

A train came in and they sat side by side. Harry had Richard's suitcase on his lap. Harry said, 'How were the exams?'

'Oh all right,' Richard said. He blushed. 'Are we going away these holidays?'

'I don't think so.'

'Mummy said I might go to America.'

'Did she write?' What else did she say?' They were

travelling down a slope and the coaches shook. The straps moved like pointers on a seismograph.

'Just that, really. What's she doing?'

'Her father's ill.'

'D'you think I could go there?'

They got out and went up in a slow lift like a tide. In the street there were bright shop windows with names in rectangles on top of them. Harry bought a paper. There was a headline *Regent's Park Murder – New Clue*. Richard said 'What happened about the satellite?'

'I don't know,' Harry said. 'They start these stories and stop them.'

'It might have gone off,' Richard said.

They walked through a quiet street with houses in small blocks with gardens. There was the gate of the semi-detached house with gables. Harry said 'You could stay a bit with Aunt Lydia in the country, would you like that?' 'Oh quite,' Richard said. 'Helen will be coming each day, you like her, don't you?' 'Oh yes,' Richard said. He walked behind Harry up the steps.

Helen was in the hall. She was straight and neat with her clothes fitting like a telescope. She said 'Hullo Richard, had a good term?' Richard kept his cap on. They went up the stairs and into the bedroom with the cactus and the model of the Taj Mahal. 'Your cap,' Helen said. Richard bent down by the cactus and touched it. 'There's a bit broken,' he said. He took his cap off. Helen opened the suitcase. Harry said 'I'll be downstairs.'

He went to the sitting-room and picked up the *Radio Times*. There was a picture on the cover of a straw hat with a hole in it and a man looking through with his thumbs in his ears. Harry threw it away. He saw a packet of Jenny's cigarettes on the mantelpiece. He said 'This is awful.' Through the window there was a plane tree coming into leaf with its branches misty. He ran up the stairs and shouted 'Richard, let's see if there's a treat that we can do!'

A tall boy with long black hair sat with his feet up silhouetted against green grass and a line of elm trees in the park. He was stretched between two green straight-backed wood-and-iron chairs. He wore a short beige corduroy jacket and dark tapering trousers. He had a green felt hat tipped over his eyes. The grey paths of the park criss-crossed into the distance with trails of walkers moving towards horizons. A clump of trees was fringed with cherry blossom. Daffodils were in the milky air.

A group of boys approached. They spread out in an inverted V like a battle formation. They wore light-coloured jackets cut away at the front. One carried a hat-box. They moved across the green spaces calling to one another. One yodelled and fell on his face with his head in his arms. The boy behind stepped on him. They reached the boy sitting with his feet up who appeared to be asleep. They stood with their hands in their pockets facing outwards in different directions. One took out a comb. He had long auburn hair brushed up at the sides.

The boy with the green hat swung his legs to the ground, knocking a chair over. He pretended to kick it, swinging his instep and stopping just short. He had two unused theatre tickets stuck in the band of his hat. He set off towards the park gates with the rest of the group following. They bumped and flicked their feet at each other like footballers. The boy with the hat-box walked in the middle.

In the road they ran for a moving bus and caught it swinging themselves up by the steel bar and jostling on the platform. The last one ran with prancing steps like a clown. They dragged him on. The conductor was black: he said 'Inside please.' They copied him – 'Inside your insaide. Pliss. Piss.' They pushed up the steps and the boy who had yodelled fell down again and they stepped over him. On the top they fell into seats on either side of the gangway and turned inwards. The boy who had fallen down came slowly along the gangway clasping the lower part of his stomach. The tall boy pulled him so that he fell over the back of a seat and stared up into the faces of two smartly dressed women. The women looked out of the window.

The bus went into a district of brightly lit shops with advertisingboards across their tops like lids. The boys got off. They ran down a side street into an avenue with ghostly trees. There was a brick wall with an alleyway through it and steps going down to a canal. The water had semi-circular patches of scum on it. A railway bridge crossed it making a dark cavern criss-crossed with girders and supports like funnels. This stretched back from the canal with a floor of stones and broken glass and glint of oil. The boys sat down.

The boy with the hat-box untied the string and

opened it slightly. There was a scuffling sound. He put a hand in and pulled out a duck, held by its neck and breast. The duck's feathers were a mottled brown. Its head was narrow and soft like fur. It struggled, getting one wing opened and clawing with its feet. The boy pressed it to him. It became rigid, with its tail upwards and its neck flattened against its back.

The tall boy knelt and pulled at its outer wing. The bones and feathers stretched. At the end there were feathers coloured with strips of bright blue with a black bar on either side and white tips. The kneeling boy took one of these and pulled it. The duck clawed. The feather came out. The boy holding the duck bent down and put his fingers over the two small holes of its nose on the upper beak. The kneeling boy plucked the coloured feathers until they were all out. They shone like enamel.

The boy let the duck go. It waddled towards the canal. A train went past on the bridge behind with a rush of steam. The tall boy had taken the theatre tickets out of his hat and was fixing in two of the bright feathers. The others watched him. The duck had turned and began coming towards them again, squawking. A boy picked up a stone and threw it. It skimmed on the water. The duck slipped on the mud and fell on its breast. The boys stood up.

The duck seemed to have lost its balance. It circled with its wing on one side like a slowing top, then fell into the canal. It flapped in the scum.

The boys ran for the alley and disappeared up the steps. There was a rush of feet behind the brick wall.

Their heads appeared in a row above the parapet by the railway bridge – the tall boy wearing his hat with the feathers in it. Then there appeared above the parapet the wheels of a tradesman's bicycle with a carrier at the front and a plate with white lettering below the cross-bar. It came sailing over. The boys' heads disappeared. The bicycle hit the bank and ricocheted with its front wheel spinning into the canal. It sank. The duck bounced on the ripples.

Lord Sykes sat behind his red leather desk and smoothed a hand over the top sheet of a pile of papers and blew on it. He leaned back in a swivel chair and read several pages, added a note at the bottom, initialled it, put the papers in a dispatch-box, took some more from the pile, smoothing them. He swivelled sideways and stretched his legs out with one finger up his cheek where his profile rested. A buzzer sounded on his desk. He said 'Yes?' A voice said 'Lord Sidney, sir.' He swung himself back and said 'Thank you.' He put the papers into a drawer in the leg of his desk and locked it with a key from his watch-chain.

He was standing when the old man with white hair came in. He stepped round his desk with his hand out and a bright smile. He said 'Edward!' Lord Sidney had been shown in by a young man in a black coat and striped trousers: he waited till the man had closed the door behind him. 'I'm – being – inconvenient,' Lord Sidney said, taking Lord Sykes's hand and staring into his blue eyes with his small deep black ones. 'Not at all,' Lord Sykes said. They went on holding hands. 'Sit down Edward,' Lord Sykes said. 'We can talk?' Lord Sidney said; 'no microphones?' He lowered himself into an armchair and put his silver-knobbed stick between his knees. Lord Sykes sat in the swivel chair and leaned with his elbows on the desk. 'None of your young men going over to Moscow?' Lord Sidney shouted.

'I'm sorry you've come all this way,' Lord Sykes said.

'I'm not trying to find out,' Lord Sidney said. 'I just want to know the danger.'

'Our information is, none.'

'Why don't we publish?'

'Half the story would be confusing,' Lord Sykes said. 'The whole story of course we don't know. It takes time.'

'Let me get this,' Lord Sykes said. 'One of these things has gone off where it shouldn't.'

'There's been some miscalculation,' Lord Sykes said. 'No one expected there wouldn't, sooner or later.'

'What do the Americans say?'

'The point is, it's a miscalculation within controlled limits.'

'I'm not trying to get it out of you!' Lord Sidney shouted.

'It's been common knowledge that the Americans have wanted to give the impresssion that they've had these things in orbit for some time. You knew this,' Lord Sykes said.

'But have they or haven't they?'

'We know our own dispositions of course.'

Lord Sidney chewed the inside of his lip. He made a wheezing sound. 'I told you,' he said.

'We knew something,' Lord Sykes said, 'our instruments tell us.'

'We've known it for days!' Lord Sidney shouted.

Lord Sykes lowered his head and looked at a sharpened unused pencil held horizontally between two fingers. He said 'We're grateful to the press.'

'Let us know if you want any information,' Lord Sidney said. He opened and shut his mouth. 'But action! decision!' He banged his hand on his stick. 'Trust the people!' His eyes went misty.

'The policy is to wait for reports,' Lord Sykes said.

Lord Sidney struggled to his feet. He pressed himself round on the arm of his chair. Lord Sykes stood by him. 'I'm an old man,' Lord Sidney said. Lord Sykes pressed a buzzer. 'I'm thinking of you, Benjamin!' Lord Sidney said. He took hold of Lord Sykes's arm. The young man in striped trousers came in. 'Look after yourself' Lord Sidney shouted. He went to the door.

When he was alone again Lord Sykes stood with one thumb in his waistcoat pocket and a leg bent at the knee. He looked at the carpet which was pale beige, and soft. The walls of the room had a strip of brown panelling round the bottom, and above it yellow wallpaper with spaced-out stars. The ceiling was encrusted with plasterwork and from it hung a light in a white bowl with chains. There was a bookcase with a glass-covered front and a map on an easel. The desk had a huge silver inkstand and some reference books in a frame. Through the window was the cornice of another heavy, smooth stone building.

Lord Sykes took his small gold penknife out of his

pocket and squatted above the carpet where there was a stain. He blew on it and brushed it with the back of his hand. He shaved off the top of the pile carefully.

Annie entered an enormous square building and stood in a marble hall. A porter dressed like a bus conductor poked his head out of a glass box. Annie said 'I wanted to find out about some work.' 'Work?' the porter said. 'I'm told you have jobs for people who want to do something – for refugees or famine relief or something like that.' 'Do you want Mrs Murchison?' the porter said. 'Do I?' Annie said. 'Up the stairs and room 137 on the right.' The porter pointed.

At the top of the stairs there were swing doors leading to a long stone passage. The doors swung behind Annie with a crash. A man appeared and said 'Can you be quiet?' Annie turned to him. He was a short round man with spectacles: he had a badge in his coat lapel of three arrows pointing upwards. 'I'm sorry,' Annie said. 'We're having a prayer meeting,' the man said. 'I was looking for room 137,' Annie said. 'You've come the wrong way.' 'Please can you tell me the right way?' Annie said.

She went back past the stairs and along another stone passage. Inside room 137 was a woman with grey hair behind a typewriter. Annie said 'I wanted to find out about some work, a job with refugees or something like that.'

'Who was it you wanted to see?' the typist said.

'Mrs Murchison.'

'I'm Mrs Murchison,' the typist said.

She took a file of papers from a drawer. 'What was it exactly you had in mind?'

'I wondered what you needed.'

'Perhaps I could have some particulars.' The woman took a pen, tried writing with it, shook it, tipped an inkpot, propped it with a rubber. 'Your name?'

'Anne Longley.'

'Age?'

'Twenty-seven.'

'Not *the* Anne Longley I suppose. Your profession?'

Annie looked out of the window where there was a cornice of a heavy stone building streaked with soot. She said 'Journalist.'

'Oh,' the typist said. 'I'm so sorry. Would you like to see Mr Simmonds?'

'I don't mind,' Annie said.

The typist smiled. She went out of the room. Annie sat with her hands over her bag in her lap. Her face was white. A clergyman with thick black hair came in. He said 'Miss Longley, how do you do, what can I do for you?' He sat down opposite her and leaned forward with his elbows on his knees.

'I wondered if you had any work,' Annie said, 'for people who want to do something for refugees or famine relief, or something like that.'

'Yes of course,' the clergyman said. He took the file. 'What sort of person is it for?'

'Me,' Annie said.

'Yes,' the clergyman said. He looked at the file. 'Well, we do have some posts for the World Council and Inter-

Church Aid, but of course most of these require specialist training. What was it exactly you had in mind?'

'I've had training in research work,' Annie said.

'Yes,' the clergyman said. 'Most of our jobs are on the medical side, you'll appreciate, but we do have our training schemes of course.'

'Don't you need people just to work?' Annie said. 'There's enough going on in the world.'

'We do have parties of students, but that wouldn't do.'

'Why not?'

The clergyman laughed. 'Oh, it's very rough!'

'What are your training courses?'

'I don't think we have anything at the moment,' the clergyman said.

Annie frowned so that vertical lines appeared between her eyebrows. She shivered.

The clergyman said 'Was it that you wanted to write something?'

Annie stood up. She said 'No.' She did her sudden bright smile.

'We have got your address?' the clergyman said.

'I'll write it down,' Annie said. She tore off a piece of paper. 'You can put it in that lovely big file.' She went to the door. 'Could you tell me the way out, please, coming up I got told off by a man at a prayer meeting.'

The clergyman went to the door. 'On the right,' he said. He pointed.

'You are kind!' Annie said. She went off. The clergyman watched her.

* * *

"Ullo,' Jules said, pushing his head round the door of Harry's sitting-room and finding Richard there alone above some electrical apparatus on the floor; 'your dad in, eh?' 'I don't think so,' Richard said. 'D'you know when 'e'll be back?' 'Not really,' Richard said. Jules remained half round the door as if about to fall down. Richard's apparatus was festooned with copper wire. 'Your dad said I could come round, an' I 'ave done, once or twice,' Jules said; 'what's that you've got there?' The door swung and he lurched in after it. 'A radio?"

'I'm making it,' Richards aid.

Jules squatted down. He was wearing his dark grey suit with a high-necked sweater. His hair was brushed forwards in its fringe. 'Get anything?'

'I did but it's gone,' Richard said.

'Let's try.' Jules picked up the earpiece and moved a knob in and out slowly.

'Could you pick up the satellite?' Richard said.

'Only very strong receivers.'

'What do satellites have in them?'

'Well, Jules said. He sat back cross-legged. Richard picked up the earpiece and pushed the knob. His fair hair had silver and gold mixed. 'H-bombs, I expect,' Jules said.

'Us or Russia?'

'Oh, both. One mistake and pthh –' He made a thumbs-down sign.

'But we would win?'

'Oh no one would.' Jules rocked backwards and forwards with his hands around his knees. He spoke in his deep bass voice. 'Not a hope. Finis.'

'Then why do we do it?'

'Well you can't give up,' Jules said.

'I read somewhere that the population of the world is growing so fast there'll only be room if everyone stands up or something in two hundred years.'

'Oh aye,' Jules said. 'Nature's remedy.'

'Can you make gunpowder?'

'You mean do I know how?' Jules said. 'Saltpetre and sulphur, isn't it?'

'And carbon,' Richard said. 'Can you?'

'I could,' Jules said.

The chemists won't sell them to me,' Richard said.

Jules had taken a bone-handled knife out of his pocket and was taping it against his hand. It had a bright steel blade curved against the bone.

Richard said, 'Can I see?'

'Careful,' Jules said.

'How do you use it?' Richard said. He opened it and held it like a javelin.

'Nah, from underneath, look, the soft underbelly.'

Richard doubled up with laughter. His face went red.

'Have you ever?' he said.

'Nah,' Jules said. He closed the knife. 'Saving it for the Teds. What d'you want gunpowder for?'

'Well, just experiments and things.'

'I could get it.'

'Could you?'

'Sure. But I don't know, would anyone mind?'

Richard stood up. 'Shall we go?'

'Now?' Jules said.

'I've got the money.'

Jules got to his feet. They went out into the hall. There was the smell of cooking from the back of the house. Richard opened the front door quietly. 'Your father won't mind?' Jules said. He closed the door and it bounced open again. 'Oh no,' Richard said. He was standing in the front garden looking into a purse. They went out into the road. Richard looked up and said 'Thank you, thank you very much!' Jules blushed.

Harry came out of the building with gothic-pointed windows opposite the large office block and saw a thin red-faced man who appeared to be waiting for him. He could not remember the man at first and took his offered hand and then said 'Bill, how are things, I haven't seen you recently.' 'I haven't been too good as a matter of fact,' the man said. He frowned at Harry as if trying to catch what he was saying. 'Walk with me for a bit,' Harry said. They moved along the pavement. 'I've had rather bad luck as a matter of fact,' the man said. 'What happened?' Well you know I was going to start work on Monday, well, that morning I sprained my back.' 'So what are you doing now?' Harry said. 'Well, I'm in a bit of a bother as a matter of fact.'

They walked beside a high brick wall towards a railway bridge. The sky was a deep yellow. Harry said 'We've been in trouble too, our director Father Wodehouse is ill and it looks as if we might have to pack up.' 'Oh that's a shame,' the man said. 'This is a tough job,' Harry said. There were low lines of television aerials black against the sky. 'I'd like to help you,' the man said; 'I really would.' Harry smiled. 'No I mean it, just tell me.' 'Yes I'm sure, thank you,' Harry said.

They came to a main road and a building with steps. Harry said 'I've got to go in the police station.' The man stopped. Harry went up two steps. He put a hand to his face. He said 'Bill, how are you off for money?' 'Well I've got a job next week,' the man said. 'How are you off till then?' 'You've been very good to me already,' the man said. 'Would two pounds do?' 'Oh – ' the man said.

Harry took out the money and gave it to him. He said 'This is from me, not the office.' 'You don't know what this means,' the man said. 'Do get that job,' Harry said. 'I don't know how to thank you.' 'This is very important,' Harry said; 'now, when you get the job, stick at it.'

Inside the police-station there was a counter behind which a sergeant sat by a telephone switchboard. The sergeant said 'Good morning Mr Gates.' Harry said, 'I've come about. . . .' A man in a grey suit came in carrying a file. He said 'Harry, I've been ringing you.' 'I know,' Harry said. The man stood in front of him smiling. 'Mick Jackson,' he said. 'I did go and see Mrs Jackson,' Harry said: 'Saturday was it, I've lost count of time.' He put a hand to his face. 'Oh, that's all right!' the man said. 'In the morning, early.' Harry frowned at the ceiling: 'I told her about Mick. She was all right, I'm sorry.' 'What are you sorry about?' the man said. 'Well, I haven't seen Mick,' Harry said. 'Hey, hey, we're looking after him,' the man said; 'What d'you think we do to 'em in the hostel?'

'It was good of you to take him, Charlie,' Harry said.

''E doesn't trust us,' the man said to the sergeant. ''E thinks 'e can win the war single-'anded.'

'Lone Ranger 'ere I come,' the sergeant said.

'But I will see him,' Harry said. 'There are some boys and girls who come sometimes to my house.'

'I'll tell him,' the man said.

'You should get on to that lot up Norbury Road,' the sergeant said.

Harry said, 'I've got my son home for the holidays, I'm a bit pushed.' He ran a hand through his hair. The other two watched him. 'I mean, I've got to spend some time with him.'

The others glanced at each other, then away. 'You do that Harry,' the man said. 'Father Wodehouse is sick, I hear, that's extra for you.'

'Don't you do anything with that Norbury Road lot Mr Gates,' the sergeant said.

A police inspector came in. When he saw Harry he said 'Charlie and I have just been discussing you!' He leaned over the counter towards Harry.

Harry said 'I was just coming in.'

'Giving yourself up?'

'About Mick Jackson,' Harry said.

'Section 22,' the inspector said. 'Withholding infor- mation likely to be of assistance.'

'I'm sorry I've been a bit . . .' Harry began.

'What would your lot do with information, you're illiterate!' the man in the grey suit said to the inspector.

'Gestapo that's us,' the inspector said.

'It's all right?' Harry said.

'These are low types,' the man said. He took Harry's arm. 'Come and 'ave a drink, or are you still off it?'

'Yes, but I'd like to,' Harry said.

'Isn't he wonderful?' the man said. He gazed round the room.

'Goodbye,' Harry said to the inspector.

'Cheerio, Gates,' the inspector said.

When they had gone the inspector shook his head and laughed. The sergeant wound a sheet of paper into a typewriter.

Mick Jackson went through a brightly lit entrance with the words *Albemarle Club* above in small letters like an advertisement for cosmetics. Inside was a flight of concrete steps with walls of polished slatted wood and at the top glass swing doors with shining handles. There was a sound of rubber shoes squeaking on a wooden floor. The landing smelt like a lavatory.

Mick went through a swing door on to the balcony of a gymnasium. The floor below was marked out for basketball. Three boys were kicking a ball about, heading and passing it to one another without letting it touch the ground. They wore dark sweaters and small white shorts. They leaned back and spun with the ball in front of them as if it were about to hit them in the face.

Mick crossed the landing and went through another swing door. He was wearing a blue suit with turned back cuffs, a yellow cardigan, and red bow-tie. In a passage there was a notice-board. Mick looked at a paper which was headed *Albemarle Club table tennis fixtures* with whirls and scrolls round the lettering. There was a sound of dance music, muffled, along the passage. Mick came to an open door and saw through it a monk in a black cassock alone in a room reading a comic magazine. Mick flattened himself; then stepped across the gap as if being shot at. At the end of the passage the music was like the stamp of soldiers drilling.

Through the top half of glass doors he saw girls with small brown faces and huge hair touch hands and spin in pairs like spiders. Boys stood looking into the bright lights of a juke-box. The glass of the door distorted them like water.

Mick went back along the passage. There was a room like a café with a counter of soft-drink cylinders and a coffee-machine and tables with bright red tops. As Mick came in there was a scream and a chair fell over. A group of boys sat in a circle, facing inwards. One was on the floor on his back, clutching the lower part of his stomach. Mick stopped; his hand still on the door. A tall boy with long black hair saw him. Mick came in and went to the counter. The boy lying on the floor shouted 'Peanuts!'

The boy with long hair made as if to kick the boy on the floor, pushing himself forward and flicking with his instep. The boy on the floor swung his legs upsetting another chair with a boy on it. The third boy jumped up and lifted the chair above his head. A fourth bounced his hand in front of his mouth doing a war-cry.

A man came out from behind the bar and said 'Put that chair down.' The boys paid no attention. 'This club belongs to you boys, and I'm to see you look after it.'

A boy in a jacket of black and white squares like a jockey said 'You and who else?' then buried his head on his neighbour's shoulder. 'I'm warning you, Carter,' the man said. 'Oh I say, thanks old man, what?' the tall boy said. Another boy stood to attention and made a noise like a trumpet playing the reveille. The boy on the floor dived at the legs of the one dressed like a jockey. The man walked away.

Mick ordered a soft drink at the counter. He stood with his back to the group. A boy began to sing in a slow quavering voice, 'I said goodbye to my old teddy bear.' The others listened. The tall boy tipped his chair back and looked out of the tops of his eyes at Mick. He shouted 'Two lemonades, Micky boy!' The singing stopped.

Mick said to the barman 'How much?' and pulled out a purse.

''Ow much are you, Mick?' the boy like a jockey said. He fell to his knees.

Mick moved towards the door. The tall boy put out a hand. He said 'Come 'ere, Mick.' Mick stopped. 'I'm serious,' the tall boy said. He pushed the boy next to him off his chair and offered the chair to Mick. Mick put his hands on the back of the chair. He said 'What do you want, Ken?'

The boy like a jockey said 'Woo-woo' in falsetto.

'Quiet!' the tall boy shouted. He turned back to Mick with his head on one side. 'You've got a new friend, uh?'

'What?' Mick said. He frowned.

137

'He's got money, uh?' The tall boy looked round, stretching his neck.

'Oh, 'im,' Mick said. He blushed.

'Yes, 'im, 'im,' the tall boy said. 'Got a car?'

'Consul,' Mick said.

'You been 'ome with 'im?' the boy on his knees began laughing in his falsetto. The tall boy shouted 'Tighten it!' and kicked him. The boy rolled over.

'I'm going,' Mick said.

'Nah,' the tall boy said. He put a hand on Mick's arm. 'We're your friends.' He shot out the lower part of his body and caught the boy on the floor again with his toe. 'Get us a drink, two lemons.' The boy on the floor stood up and went to the counter. 'Cigarette?' the tall boy said to Mick. He gazed round the rest of the group, nodding. The others took out packets. One was offered to Mick. Mick took a cigarette and sat on the chair next to the tall boy. They all began lighting cigarettes.

Lord Sykes waited after the last speaker had sat down, busying himself with papers on the red leather bench beside him. There was a murmur beneath the vaults of the high panelled chamber. He then stood up and stretched his neck slightly with one hand in his waist-coat pocket fingering his small gold penknife and still half turned towards the bench. He said 'I am grateful for both the restraint and resolution of the noble earl – ' then clicked himself upright suddenly like a man with tin legs ' – since I am aware of the anxiety which their lordships feel and which he has described so graphically. Often in the history of a nation – ' he waved his papers in a downwards curve ' – there is the justifiable desire of those who seek the facts, and the justifiable obligation of authority to security. But in this situation I can say both with a due sense of responsibility and yet giving all available information, that in spite of certain things that have been said this afternoon – ' he took his hand from his waistcoat and spread it against his heart ' – things that had been better left unsaid – ' there was a murmuring from the benches like furniture being moved ' – there is no cause for alarm or for dismay. Any mistakes that have occurred – and there are bound to be mistakes in such an enterprise – are of a purely technical nature. There has been no damage or danger whatsoever – ' he spaced his words out ' – to life or to property. I need say no more until reports are received. But I should like to pay tribute to the press – ' there was another murmur – ' – who have displayed good sense and responsibility in this matter. And to add just this.'

He put his papers down on the bench beside him. He stood with his arms hanging at his sides. Then he seemed to raise himself on his toes. A peculiar hush came over the room. The man with knee-breeches stopped whispering by the door. An old man picked up his earphone.

'In these days of affluence and security there is one great truth that is tended to be forgotten – that the life of every great nation is bound up at its heart with the spirit of exploration and experiment. Today we stand on the edges of new worlds and new techniques. In every endeavour there is risk; and in great endeavours the greater risks and the greater results of failure. What we are trying to do – we and our great allies with whom we stand or fall – is nothing less than the safe-guarding of the whole free world. The freedom is threatened with gigantic forces of persuasion. These forces possess techniques of which our ancestors only dreamed. We ourselves have to make use of these tech-niques or be defeated.

'There are a few voices raised in this country today – voices even raised in another place not far from here – who would have us believe that these risks are irrespon-sible, that they are a betrayal of man's role as arbiter of life on this planet. I would say that such an attitude is a betrayal. I believe that man as we know him is given the obligation to act as the Creator's viceroy on this planet – that by his brain and energies he is called upon to order Creation. To do this he has to strive, to put himself against the unknown and intractable. He also has to suffer disappointment and sometimes pain. But it is only by the acceptance of every new challenge that he will do what his creator has demanded of him.

'Today we have what might be called the total chal-lenge, together with the total answer to it. The last war was fought with unprecedented horror. Such a war must never be fought again. But the only thing that will stop war is the power of something greater than war – some-thing that will prevent war because by its own immedi-ate threat it will make war irrelevant. For what else could prevent war – other than a power which, by its threat, could conceivably be worse than war?

'Today we have this power. On the one hand we have the certainty of these horrors coming to pass – the continuation of old national wars fought for glory or for pride. On the other hand we have the weapons which can face this challenge and defeat it. We have the choice. We know that there will be setbacks, sacrifices. But are we therefore to flee to the old helplessness and illusion? Or are we to go forward, accepting with courage the role that destiny has given us, to be the peacemakers, the arbiters, for this generation? I would not be the one to say we had lacked courage. In the days to come, may we remember this?'

Lord Sykes sat down. Two reporters moved quickly from the gallery at the end of the long chamber. There was a murmur *yeah yeah yeah* from the men on the benches. The man in knee-breeches began whispering again. Lord Sykes sat with his head bowed.

'No no no no!' Maurice Bloxham shouted. He clapped his hands and stepped into a circle of arc-lights. There was a man standing on a flight of steps in fifteenth century costume with a green felt hat with a feather. He turned towards Maurice. The flight of steps ended in a platform in the air like library steps. At the top was a huge plywood model of a keyhole, resting on stilts. Beyond the keyhole, in darkness, was a hip-bath.

'Bend down!' Maurice said; 'hands on knees, peer, be surprised!' He acted each word in mime on the bare floor-boards. 'Turn, wink: make the wink *work*!' The man on the steps stood with his hands on his hips. His face was a deep red.

Maurice stepped out of the circle of light to where television cameras stood on wheels with men crouched behind them as if they were machine guns. People moved in the shadows amongst wires. There was a high ceiling with indistinct girders.

Maurice said 'Harry! glad you could come. Richard! The last time I saw you you were oh – four or five – this is the holidays, is it, how old are you?'

'Nearly eleven,' Richard said.

'It's very good of you, Maurice,' Harry said.

'Not at all,' Maurice said: 'bit of a treat, what, seeing the other half. Try it again!' he shouted turning to the cameramen. He turned back to Richard. 'Then we'll see the real stuff. Time it!' he murmured, walking to the edge of the light. The man in the green felt hat bent down to the keyhole. He made a face of intense surprise.

On the edge of the light there was a girl standing in a white bathrobe belted at the waist. She had pale hair and a small brown face with silver eyelids and lipstick. The bathrobe ended just below her hips and was bunched outwards like a bell. Her legs were thin. She smoked a cigarette.

The man on the steps turned to the cameras with his hands on his knees. A camera swept towards him. He winked. 'Right!' Maurice shouted. He waved his hands up and down.

'What are they doing?' Richard whispered,.

'Taking it I suppose,' Harry said.

'But what's that man?'

'Robin Hood's grandmother,' Harry said. Richard began giggling with his hand to his mouth.

The man sat on the top of the steps and took off one of his pointed shoes. He massaged his toes. In the shadows Harry hobbled up and down like an old woman with a stick: he lifted the imaginary stick and drew it like a bow. Richard was red in the face with giggling. Harry let the string go and pretended it had caught him on the fingers.

Maurice said 'Five minutes!' Some of the arc-lights switched off. Maurice said to Harry 'Would he like to see the machinery, that's the interesting part, hm?' 'I'm sure,' Harry said. Richard had his back to them, blowing his nose. Two men moved about the floor with a tape measure. 'This is Richard Gates,' Maurice said. 'Hullo Richard!' a camera-man said. 'Could you show him –' Maurice said.

Harry stayed by Maurice on the edge of the light. Richard climbed on a trolley. Harry said 'How have you been, Maurice?' 'Fine, did you get home all right?' Maurice said. 'Oh, that night, yes,' Harry said. The girl in the bathrobe was talking to a man in tartan trousers: she had one arm crossed in front of her holding the elbow of the hand with the cigarette. 'How's – er – what's her name?' Maurice said. 'Who?' Harry said. 'Your wife,' Maurice said. He put a hand up to his forehead. Richard had left the camera and was being taken behind a glass panel where people sat by tables of instruments: his fair head moved along a grey and white background. 'How's Jenny, have you seen her?' Harry said. 'Oh yes, yes,' Maurice said. The girl in the bathrobe laughed, flicking the ash from her cigarette. 'All right all right!' Maurice shouted. The arc-lights came on.

Richard came back and stood by Harry. He whispered

'Super control room, hundreds of knobs.' The cameras were wheeled towards the hip-bath which stood on linoleum against a backdrop of a blue sea and palm-trees. 'They've got six pictures, it's all automatic, huge wires and thousands of volts.' 'But what are they doing?' Harry said. The girl in the bathrobe had stepped into the circle of light. 'They're rehearsing,' Richard said. 'It's all dreams,' Harry said. 'But what are the rays, do they go outwards, in all directions, all the time?' Richard said. 'Yes,' Harry said. The girl was putting on high-heeled shoes. She stood at the end of the hip-bath and put her hands on its rim. Richard said 'Gosh!' The girl bent over the bath, lowering her waist. The man in tartan trousers pulled at her bathrobe behind. The girl blinked her eyes very fast. Maurice stood in front of her. He clicked his fingers. The girl looked into the camera and pursed her mouth into an open 'O'.

'Do they go right through you?' Richard said.

'Yes,' Harry said. The camera began moving in like a machine-gun.

Annie sat on a beach by a breakwater where waves came in in long white lines ceaselessly. They washed against wooden posts with weeds and limpets. The sand glistened. Small white stones were scattered over it with holes scooped out by water. Flocks of birds moved up and down with the waves.

Annie leaned with her head against a post. Her hair on one side was blown flat by wind. She rolled sideways with her hands in her lap and her head on the sand. The surface was damp. She made a small hollow with her cheekbone, and the sand got into her mouth and tasted dead. An image came into her mind of a wounded horse with its neck stretched out and its body swollen above it.

She drew her knees up so that her legs and arms made an enclosure within which her head was protected. She opened one eye and saw close to it a patch of sand like the floor of a tent. The wind blew over the top of her body, and she herself was inside.

There seemed to be some secret in this hollow. It was like a valley hidden by mountains – one of those valleys in story-books cut off from the rest of the world and in the depths of which was a civilization of calm and happy men. The inhabitants of the valley never went out, and no trespassers from outside came to disturb them. Then one day there was an accident – a plane-crash or refugees from war – and there came a small group, perhaps no more than two, climbing through the snow of high passes where mist wrapped round the stones like music; and they descended at night to the foothills. Then in the morning they woke in a glittering world with strange people watching them; and they looked across the valley with its fields of yellow flowers and towers like the down-turned cups of bells.

Harry and she had been walking like this that day – there was a path in the fold of her skirt down which they had slid – a sunny day on an English summer road with the hawthorn out and the smell of dust wet for cleaning – and Harry had said – this was the secret of the valley – 'You only know it for a moment, this is what time is' – standing on the opposite side of the road, not touching, separated from her as in some almost motionless dance. Where the sand of the valley lay against her skirt they had sat on the edge of the fields and looked towards the towers. 'But how do we remember?' Annie had said. She had tried to memorize the scene, taking a last look as if from a moving train and then turning away and thinking – But now it has gone – and looking back to imprint the details but with what she had remembered now itself dissolving, so that in trying to keep it she lost even what she had. Then what was it? she thought. What is it?

A gust of wind blew over her back. It felt like the tide coming in. At the end of the valley there was a mountain which was shaped like a man's face staring upwards at the sky. The head rose in a curve of black curly hair to a forehead-plateau and a straight nose and lips and chin pressed close together. The eyes were closed. The whole ridge seemed to be a fallen statue with a man imprisoned in it. It strained at the sky. Annie moved, yearning for it. The feeling of her body came back to her against the wet earth. The man's head was in her lap; she cradled it. The sand in her mouth was rough and tasteless.

She opened one eye and there was the curve of her skirt and beyond it the noise of the sea. She drew her arms to her breast: the head was not there. She stretched her legs and the wind came in and she saw the sand and the milky white light and the waves coming in ceaselessly. The birds were standing facing out to sea and their reflections shone in the wetness. Her head was lying curiously close to the earth and her body seemed swollen above it.

Lord Sidney stood in a large office with two beige-coloured walls and on the third a spidery modern fresco and the fourth made entirely of glass. Through this window could be seen the spires and skyscrapers of central London: the fresco opposite reflected this scene but in a swirl of charcoal as if the whole city were in flames. Lord Sidney walked across the room with his cautious tread and opened a door dramatically. There was no one there. He moved back to his desk and shouted into a box 'Where is he?' Jules's head appeared round the door behind and said 'Hullo Grandpa!' 'Wake up!' Lord Sidney shouted into the box. He began crossing the room again, holding on to bits of furniture. He said 'Jules!' taking Jules's elbow where there was a leather patch. He stared up at Jules whose chin was on a level with his forehead. 'Where've you been?'

'Talking to your secretary,' Jules said in his deep voice.

Lord Sidney began crossing the room for the fourth time. He dragged past the swirl of burning London. He said 'What've you been saying?'

'She's good-looking,' Jules said.

'What?' Lord Sidney shouted. He sat behind a desk and waved Jules to a chair at forty-five degrees to it.

'Asked 'er if she'd like to get on in the firm by goin' out with the old man's grandson,' Jules said. He rubbed his hands.

'How's the work?' Lord Sidney shouted.

'Well I was going to ask you,' Jules said. He leaned with his elbows on his knees. 'I've been thinking, as a matter of fact.'

'Don't strain yourself' Lord Sidney said. He laughed.

Jules pursed his lips. He said 'I want to leave.'

'That's what you've been thinking?' Lord Sidney said.

'But the point is, I don't exactly know what I want to do.'

'I see.'

'It sounds rather silly,' Jules said. He looked up. 'I want to go to Australia.'

'Well, you're not doing that!' Lord Sidney shouted. He held a pen vertically against the desk and slid his fingers down it.

'Why not?' Jules said.

'What are you going to do for money – '

'I was going to ask you – ' Jules began.

'I'm sure!'

Jules paused. 'I can pay my way, but to start me off – '

'Just a moment,' Lord Sidney said. He sat with his chin jutting out. He turned the pen over and put the nib against the desk. 'You want to throw away the education and job I've provided for you. . . .'

'I'd pay you back,' Jules said. He looked at his hands between his knees.

'I've been watching your work here,' Lord Sidney said. He scratched the pen against the desk. 'Don't think it's for my own good I employ you. As far as I'm concerned you'd be better away. But I've got a responsibility for you. I kept your father and I'll keep you. If you don't like the job, I might find another.'

'Oh, it's a rotten job,' Jules said loudly. 'Why do you print some of that stuff?'

Lord Sidney said 'I'll make it plain what I mean. Many mistakes are made because people don't make plain what they mean.' His small black eyes had gone smoky. 'You've got to face the fact that you've got a second-rate intelligence and third-rate ability to apply it to hard work. Given perseverance you might get a decent position in business. But you have no talent for making a success on your own.'

Jules said 'Hm,' and rubbed the palms of his hands together.

'I believe you have a high opinion of yourself,' Lord Sidney said, 'though why has never been explained to me.' He stood and walked a few steps with his hands behind his back. 'From my reports it appears you spend most of your time hanging around cafés with bearded beatniks.'

'Oh really!' Jules said.

'Yes?' Lord Sidney shouted.

'That's silly.'

Lord Sidney faced Jules with his legs apart and rose on his toes. 'I'm interested you think that. You're ready to take my money but not my advice.'

'I mean about beatniks.'

'Is it or is it not a fact that you live in a house full of degenerates and non-whites?'

'It's all I can afford,' Jules said. He looked up. 'I've got friends who'll help me if you don't.'

'Who?'

'Quite well-off people,' Jules said.

149

'I'm only interested in facts,' Lord Sidney said. 'Their names.'

'Well there's a chap called Harry Gates,' Jules said.

'Gates,' Lord Sidney said. He sat at the desk and wrote it down.

'And Father Patterson,' Jules said. 'He's quite well known.'

'A priest?'

'Yes.'

'You've been got at by priests?'

'I met him.'

'I see,' Lord Sidney said. He wrote again. 'You realize of course my position with the Roman Church?'

'He's an Anglican,' Jules said.

'No man who calls himself father is an Anglican,' Lord Sidney said. His eyes had become sharp and bright. 'They know the stand I and my papers take against foreign elements. You'd be a feather in their cap. Always look for the pattern. Analyse and clarify.'

'It's not like that, Grandpa,' Jules said as if to a child.

'They can't attack me so they attack my dependents,' Lord Sidney said. He smiled. 'Idleness and bad company open the door to priests! They've played on your weaknesses. Your father was the same – a man with a crack in him.' He leaned forward over the desk.

'Ah,' Jules said, like a groan.

'He took to drink, perverts, because he hadn't got the guts. And you want to follow him.' He leaned back. 'But I'll stand by you. You'll stay and work here. We'll make a man of you.'

'I wasn't thinking of going just yet,' Jules said.

'I'll see what I can do,' Lord Sidney said, 'though details of appointments are in the hands of my managers.' He picked up a block of paper and threw it back in the same place. 'I'm glad you came. Always come to the top. Always clarify.' He seemed waiting for Jules to go. Jules sat and stared at his hands.

'Are you coming to my dinner?' Lord Sidney shouted. He stood and ushered Jules towards the door. 'See my secretary.' He put a hand on his arm. 'I looked after your father!'

'I saw Mummy the other day,' Jules said.

Lord Sidney's eyes went smoky again. He went into the passage and into another beige room with a secretary. He shouted 'Give me the dinner!'

'The dinner, sir?' the secretary said.

'Wake up!' Lord Sidney shouted. He picked a sheaf of papers and thumbed through it. 'Fit in Mr Cavendish.'

'Oh thanks,' Jules said.

'She'll tell you,' Lord Sidney said. 'Goodbye then, Jules!' He held his arm and did the bright stare that winked on and off like a car indicator.

When he had gone Jules ran his hand through his hair and said 'Cor!' The secretary said 'Thursday next.' She wore a white blouse with a string of pearls and had a brown face in ash-blonde hair. 'Where do you go in the evenings?' Jules said. '8.30 for 9, evening dress,' the secretary said. 'Take you to somethin' you 'aven't seen before,' Jules said. 'I'll send you an invitation,' the secretary said. 'What're you frightened of, think I'd 'urt you?' Jules said.

* * *

Harry stood in a high-roofed building with a stage at one end and green tubular chairs around the walls and large lights like an operating theatre. There was a game of table tennis in one corner and darts half-way up and a boy playing jazz on an upright piano. Harry was talking to a short fragile-looking boy who wore dark glasses and a brown felt hat. The boy was saying 'But it's not fair on you.' 'Oh good heavens!' Harry said. The boy turned to the room and shouted 'Can we have quiet, please?' No one listened. 'Can we have a bit of hush?'

The piano stopped. There were about twenty girls and ten boys. They dragged chairs into a semicircle round the stage where Harry and the boy stood. The girls wore bright summer dresses with flared skirts and cardigans: the boys dark suits with white shirts, some with pleats, and narrow ties.

The fragile-looking boy took off his hat and began: 'I think this is a pretty poor attendance. I'm not grumbling, but I organize this club and then you don't turn up. I don't do it for myself, you know.'

They sat in rows and watched him. A big boy with red hair said 'We've turned up.'

'But what about the others?' Two girls at the back began giggling. 'I don't see what's funny in it.'

Harry sat facing them on the edge of the stage. There was one girl he had not seen before, with silver-coloured hair like a fountain.

'Anyway,' the fragile boy went on, 'what I've arranged is, an outing to Westminster Abbey on Saturday, badminton and table tennis on Tuesday, and Mr Gates has

152

kindly said we can have our dance at his house. Now who wants to go to Westminster Abbey?'

No one moved.

'This is a church club you know,' the boys aid. 'You must like something other than jiving.'

'I'll go,' the red-haired boy said. He raised his hand which was holding the hand of a pretty dark girl beside him.

'What time on Saturday?' a boy with spectacles said.

'Leave three-thirty, arrive four, refreshments four-thirty, you'll be back before six, it won't kill you.'

Two more girls put up their hands.

'How many want to come to the dance?'

They all put up their hands.

'Is that all right, Mr Gates?'

'Yes,' Harry said.

'I'll give out the tickets this evening. Would you like to say something, Mr Gates?'

Harry climbed from the stage. He looked at a far corner of the ceiling. He put a hand to his coat lapel and pulled it out of shape. He said 'This is the time in the Church's year between Easter and Whitsun, when what happened was this – each person was given the power in his own heart to know truth and to do it, in what is called his conscience. Before, people had had to be taught some sort of rules and stick to them, but after Whitsun they knew that if they did what they thought right, then God would lead them to do what he thought right.' At the corner of the ceiling there was a skylight with a rope hanging down to within about eight feet of the floor. 'This is very important,' Harry said. He hitched up his lapel. 'And the chance to do right is not only in us but in the world. If we do right, then right things happen in the world. The two things depend on each other. We don't know how, but like science, we know it works.' He looked at the rows of attentive faces. 'I won't go on any more now, but if anyone wants to talk about it I'd be glad.' He walked backwards to the stage and hoisted himself up and sat.

'Thank you, Mr Gates,' the fragile-looking boy said. 'Now we have jiving.'

There was a blast from a gramophone. The noise went through the hall like strands of wire. Chairs were pulled back and dancers began clicking in clockwork time. They were mostly girls, spinning and flicking their wrists as if making horses' heads with shadows. Harry saw Mick Jackson come in at the door. He was wearing his blue suit with the turned-back cuffs. The beat of the music bounced off the walls. There was the girl with silver-coloured hair with her skirt going outwards from the waist like a bell. Her thin legs were like clappers.

The boy with red hair came up to Harry. He said 'I was interested in that.' He still held the hand of the dark girl who peered at Harry with her cheek on the boy's shoulder. He said 'But what about the people who think they're right and aren't?'

'There have to be some rules,' Harry said. 'But I think those people do in fact stop themselves knowing what they should know, they cut themselves off and won't think or use their eyes.' The noise from the gramophone

154

was so great he had to yell at the boy and girl a few inches from him.

'Is it their fault?'

'In some sense, yes,' Harry shouted.

'What sense?'

'At one or two moments of their lives,' Harry shouted. He saw the silver-coloured girl dancing close to him. She had a pale mouth and eyes like dust. 'Of course it's very difficult,' he shouted.

'You think if we all tried hard we should all think the same?'

'No, all think differently but should make up the whole,' Harry shouted.

The record changed. There was a slower, sadder thump. The red-haired boy and girl went to dance. Mick Jackson was standing in a group. The fragile-looking boy had put on his brown felt hat and was peering through his dark glasses at an electrical connection. Harry shouted 'There are a few new ones tonight, Paul.' 'Yes, Mick Jackson, I'm glad to see,' Paul said. 'And one or two girls,' Harry shouted. 'Are there?' Paul said. He looked up at the bright, spinning dresses: 'Yes, we're doing well, considering.'

Jerril stood by the window of Lydia's London drawing-room that looked out on a neat square of Georgian houses. He was reading a copy of *The Times*. There were headlines – *Responsibility and Sacrifice* – *Lord Sykes's Statement of Faith*. Lydia sat on a sofa with her feet up. Her face was greasy except for dark eyebrows which were in straight lines like her mouth. Jerril read from the paper – ' "I believe that man as we know him is given the obligation to act as the Creator's viceroy on his planet".' He put the paper down. 'I like "man as we know him", don't you? I can see Benjy being viceroy of a lot of things, a sort of Fid. Def. Ind Coope.'

Lydia's shoulders shook slightly, though her eyebrows and mouth remained straight.

' "The role that destiny has given us",' Jerril read. 'I suppose it gave him that dreadful Peter Poole.'

'Oh Jerril!' Lydia exclaimed. She stretched her eyes and bit her lip like a young girl.

'Have you heard Leo's story about the homosexuality bill?' Jerril said.

'I can't bear it!' Lydia exclaimed.

Jerril moved round the room. In an alcove there were shelves with small china figures of negroes kneeling with their hands held out, negroes inlaid in ivory boxes and in coloured prints, with captions beneath them and dates of the agitation about the slave trade. There was a recurrent caption 'Oh pity me . . .!'

'I've already got a headache!' Lydia said.

'Put your head back,' Jerril said. She laid her head on the arm of the sofa. He stood behind her and put his fingers on her temples. He stroked them gently. He said. 'They were all having dinner at Pitt's one night, and Malcom was talking about the homosexuality bill in his dreadful slow voice, and Benjy was saying homosexuality with a long "o" and Malcom interrupted him hŏmo, hŏmo, and Benjy said "I thought it came from the Latin hōmo, a man", and Malcom said "No, it comes from the Greek hŏmos, the same", and Benjy said "But isn't that a man?" '

Lydia opened her mouth and shrieked. Jerril stroked her. Lydia said 'Leo has such dreadful stories!'

'I'm waiting for him to get a patient in the palace.'

'They look so stable.'

'Before the horse has gone,' Jerril said. His hand moved beneath her rather masculine jaw. He held her mouth closed. Her eyes were shut. He said 'And what about Harry?'

Lydia made a murmuring noise.

'He's supposed to pick up boys from his clubs and take them home.'

'Oh, Jerril!' Lydia exclaimed.

'He had one for the weekend the other day.'

'How do you know?'

'All Christianity's a failure to get past the homo-sexuality stage.'

'But not Harry!'

'Why not Harry?' Jerril said. He massaged her throat. The corners of her mouth were dragged down. 'Not Harry, what?' He bent over her.

'Oh that's better,' Lydia said.

'He lost Melissa.'

'Harry's a saint,' Lydia said.

'Little brother's a saint,' Jerril said. He squeezed her throat. 'Doesn't little sister know what little saints do to each other?'

Lydia's shoulders shook. She opened her mouth and breathed through it heavily. 'Hm?' Jerril said.

'Little sister knows,' Lydia said in a baby voice.

Jerril touched her windpipe. She suddenly made a gurgling sound. She opened her eyes and looked straight at him. He took his hand away. She sat up and touched her hair. Jerril's eyes went into rectangular slits with the lids parallel. Lydia arranged a brooch on her coat, looking down with her neck wrinkled. Jerril hunched his shoulders. He moved about the room.

'They can come in here,' Harry said, moving through his house like an estate agent with Helen following him; 'there won't be more than forty, they'll only dance.' 'Isn't it supposed to be a church club?' Helen said. 'Oh you must have dancing,' Harry said; 'dancing's important.' 'Well I do think it's good of you to let them have your house.' 'It's the only way to make friends,' Harry said.

He went into the kitchen and began opening and shutting drawers. He found glasses and put them out. Helen said 'Lemonade and buns for forty then.'

Harry sat down. 'It's no good preaching. I wonder why we open our mouths.' He watched Helen cutting slices of bread. 'You see, you don't talk much, Helen.'

Helen blushed. She was in profile to him with her straight jersey and skirt.

'Do you have troubles, Helen? You'd never tell us.'

'Don't be too sure,' Helen said.

'We're so awful with our troubles,' Harry said. He was astride a chair facing the back with his arms along the top. 'You're worth the lot of us, Helen.'

'Why do you think I'm different?' Helen said. She

reached into a cupboard with her back to him and banged plates about.

Richard came in. He said 'Oh sorry' and began to go out. Harry said 'Don't go.' Richard stood with his hands over the front of his trousers. 'There's a party tonight with the boys and girls, do you want to come?'

'Teddy boys?' Richard said.

'No.'

'What are they doing?'

'Dancing mostly.'

'Oh blast, no,' Richard said.

Beneath his hands there was a burnt patch with blackened edges on his trousers. Harry leaned forward and touched it. Helen said 'What's that?' 'Oh nothing,' Richard said. 'Is it those chemicals?' Helen said. 'What chemicals?' Harry said. 'Oh just chemicals,' Richard said. 'I do wish you'd look at them, Harry,' Helen said.

Harry said 'When I was at school we used to put chemicals in the petrol tank of the bus that brought visiting sports teams, and it all blew up at the end of the drive.'

'Gosh, did it?' Richard said.

'Well, it stopped.'

'You better go up and change those trousers,' Helen said.

When Richard had gone Helen said 'That was a nasty burn.'

'I will do something,' Harry said. He ran his hand through his hair. 'There's so much!'

'It's not easy for Richard,' Helen said. She was buttering bread methodically.

'He probably doesn't like the boys and girls coming to the house,' Harry said.

'It's more than that.'

Harry said 'What?'

'Well,' Helen said.

'Do say, Helen.'

'I don't think I'm much use here.'

'But you are!' Harry said; 'I don't know what I'd do!'

Helen had her back to him and was scraping knives up from a drawer. She said 'You will talk to him about his chemicals, won't you?'

Harry said 'You don't want to stop coming, do you?'

'I didn't mean that,' Helen said.

Harry rested his head on the back of the chair. He said 'I dread this evening. Why do I dread it so much?'

Father Patterson was writing a letter:

Dear Harry,

I was suggesting the other day to Jules Cavendish that he should meet you, when he said he already had. This is a coincidence! I'm sure you're the person for him. I've had him here twice, but a priest can't do much at this stage. As you probably know, his father is dead and his mother's a dipsomaniac and the main influence in his life seems to be his grandfather, Lord Sidney, who I suppose is a monster. What he wants is to get right away, but he thinks he'll be letting his grandfather down. In the meantime he's in for all sorts of nonsense.

I wonder if you could have a go at him. I know he

likes you (I gather he met you in some low dive) and
has been round to you once or twice, but I gather he
hasn't talked much. I do hope you don't mind my
suggesting this.

Father Patterson heard a telephone ringing. He waited
to see if anyone would answer it, then went down to
the first floor. A woman's voice said 'Can I speak
to Father Patterson?'

'Speaking.'

'Father Patterson? Oh I'm sorry to bother you, but
I'm making enquiries about a young man called Jules
Cavendish, I wondered if you knew him.'

'Who is speaking?'

'You won't know me I'm afraid. I'm speaking on
behalf of certain relatives.'

'Yes, I know him,' Father Patterson said.

'I'm so glad. Can you tell me, have you seen him
recently?'

'Yes,' Father Patterson said. 'I'm afraid I must ask you
who you are.'

'Thank you so much, Father Patterson.'

'Is there anything wrong with Jules?'

'Oh no, thank you, Father Patterson.' There was a
click and the dialling tone.

Father Patterson went back to his room. He re-read
his letter. He wrote:

I should very much like to see you. Could you spare
a moment one day? I expect Richard is home for the
holidays, and you'll be busy. But let me know.

161

He signed the letter and sealed it. He was going down to the letter-box in the hall when the telephone began ringing again. A man's voice said 'Can I speak to Father Patterson?'

'Speaking.'

'Oh Father Patterson, my name is Ian Arbuthnot of the *Evening Post*, I wonder if you could help me, we're doing certain features on the practical aspects of religion and we wondered – '

'Who did you say?' Father Patterson said.

'Ian Arbuthnot of the London *Evening Post*.'

'Oh yes,' Father Patterson said.

'We're doing certain articles on the practical aspects of religion, and I'm told you do social welfare work in North London, is that correct?'

'Yes,' Father Patterson said.

'I wondered if I might come and see you.'

'Why?'

'Well, to get some facts.'

'Yes, do come round,' Father Patterson said.

There was a silence. 'What?' the voice said.

'What time would suit you?'

'Oh that's very good of you, Father Patterson. May I ring you later and make an appointment?'

'Yes do,' Father Patterson said. There was the dialling tone.

He went to the post box and wrote on the back of the envelope *Would definitely like to see you*; then dropped the letter in. He went to the chapel. He sat in his stall and stared at a corner of the canopy above the altar. Then he knelt.

* * *

From the back garden of his house Harry listened to the music which seemed to expand and contract the walls with air-pressure. Through a lighted window he saw girls in their flowered dresses like bells; boys in a group leaning inwards over a record-player. In the garden there was a fence with a plank missing. A bed of roses was unpruned above weeds.

At the start of the dance he had been inside. He had stood by the fragile-looking boy and said 'Everything all right, Paul?' and Paul had said 'Fine, Mr Gates.' Paul had been wearing his dark glasses and a black suit with a cream shirt and yellow tie. 'Quite a good crowd,' Harry had said. 'Yes, these dances are popular,' Paul had said. Harry had moved his foot up and down, grinning.

The walls of the neighbouring houses were black like fortresses. The moon moved behind clouds. Helen was in the kitchen talking to a girl with piled-up hair. Richard's light was on. Harry had been upstairs earlier to put on a smarter tie, and had passed Richard's closed door and had listened outside it.

The moon appeared. He saw the Great Bear and Cassiopeia, and looked for Orion. A few days ago there had been a silver speck sliding across the sky like a line being drawn and immediately rubbed out.

The music stopped. There was a noise of shouting from the front of the house. Harry went down the narrow passage that joined the back with the small front garden. There were figures by the gate. A voice shouted 'Micky boy?' and Mick Jackson's voice said 'All right, Ken.' Harry stopped. A figure staggered through the gate six boys leaned against the fence outside the gate. Mick Jackson was with them in his tight blue suit and his hair brushed up. The boy on the lawn did ghostly artificial laughter. On the far side of the road there was a group of girls in overcoats and with handkerchiefs over their heads. They held handbags in front of them like shields.

Harry walked forward. He said 'Mick, coming in?'

'Evening, Mr Gates,' Mick said. He walked through the group of boys and into the garden.

'Are those girls coming?' Harry said.

'Coming in girls?' Mick called.

A voice answered 'Yes,' faintly.

'Excuse me – ' Harry said. He went to the gate.

'Oh excuse me!' someone copied him. There was a shout of 'Teachah!' and a noise like a balloon deflating. The boy who had been on the lawn pushed his way out shouting 'Thank you!' He doubled up and ran along the road.

The girls were half-way across. The boy running suddenly screamed and did his ghostly laughter. The girls turned back, trotting on high heels and with their hands to their throats.

'Oh let them in!' Harry said.

A boy taller than the rest, not looking at Harry, said 'Is 'e talkin'?'

'What do you want?' Harry said.

'Don't you say *please*?' the tall boy said. The others stood round him, waiting.

'Are you the teacher?' another boy said.

'No,' Harry said.

164

'Don't you know what you are?' the tall boy said. They began to laugh, turning their faces away.

'Have you been invited?' Harry said. 'This is a private party.'

'Mick's invited us, haven't you, Micky boy?'

The girls were coming across the road again. They bounced slightly with one foot in front of the other like mannequins. Harry noticed the girl with silver-coloured hair. They went through in a bunch, hanging on to each other.

Harry said to Mick, 'Do you know these people? Do you want them in?'

'I do know them,' Mick said.

'I'll ask,' Harry said. He said to the boys 'Stay here.' He followed the girls into the house.

In the sitting-room there was a slow waltz playing with a saxophone and a double-bass. The lights had been switched off except for one with red cellophane round it like an artificial fire. Paul was dancing in his dark glasses with the girl with piled-up hair. Their heads were close and their bodies sloped apart like wrestlers. Harry said 'Paul, there are some boys outside who want to come in.'

Paul said 'Who?' and went to the window.

'Don't you think it's a good opportunity?' Harry said. 'I mean, we've been saying we must get people in and not just run the club for ourselves.'

'Not them,' Paul said.

'Why not? Aren't they the people we should be getting?'

'It's your house,' Paul said.

'Do you know them?'

'Yes.'

'Let's risk it,' Harry said. He found his voice trembling.

He went back to the gate. He said 'All right, be our guests, this is a church club you know.' They followed him up the steps. In the room they pushed past and made for a corner where they collapsed on each other and the floor as if in musical chairs. One clutched his stomach. The boy with dark glasses watched them. The tall boy with long hair shouted 'Pauly boy!'

Paul said 'What do you want, Ken?'

The tall boy said 'Good Pauly boy!'

'I don't want any trouble, Ken.'

The tall boy pushed at a huge white-haired boy who was on his lap. He shouted 'Get off my balls.'

'And watch your language,' Paul said.

Ken held the white-haired boy like a ventriloquist's dummy. 'Benny 'ere'd like some whisky.'

'I'll get you cokes,' Paul said.

Harry had gone into the back garden. There were squares of light from the windows. He walked round and approached the house again in the darkness beneath a tree. Through the bedroom window he could see the girls taking off their coats and tidying themselves in mirrors. The girl with silver hair was frowning. She had no make-up. Her eyebrows were dark and she had pale, clearly defined lips.

Harry had a sensation of flour and damp linen. Some of the girls were peering at a photograph of Melissa. He thought – I am remembering my dream.

Helen called – 'Harry?'

He stepped round the patches of light and joined Helen by the back door. She said 'Who are these boys?'

'I thought it'd be a good chance to make contact,' Harry said.

The troupe of girls were coming down the stairs. They held on to one another. Harry said 'In here,' cheerfully. He opened the door into the sitting-room. There was modern jazz playing. Mick Jackson stood by the gramophone. Harry went up to him. He said 'Do you like this?'

'This?' Mick said.

'I don't buy many records now,' Harry said. 'I used to. Who are the new ones now – I mean – what do you like?'

'All kinds,' Mick said. He frowned.

The boys in the corner were still in their group. The dancers kept clear of them. Above their heads was an early portrait of Melissa by Jerril, with her skin transparent.

Harry said 'How's the job, Mick?'

'Oh very good, thanks,' Mick said.

'I saw your mother again the other day.' Harry saw the boys in the corner watching him and Mick. They were laughing. 'I'm so glad it all worked out,' Harry said. He moved away.

He wandered out again into the back garden and went to the end of the lawn where there was an old sand-pit and a bench. He sat down. He said aloud 'Oh God I'm bad at it!' He stretched out his legs and kicked against something hard. It was a toy bucket with orange elephants. He picked it up. The handle was rusty. He had an impression of seaweed and the dead taste of sand.

Helen called – 'Harry!' and then – 'they're fighting!'

The sand dribbled away. He walked towards the house. The music had stopped. Groups of girls stood in the passage. The sitting-room was still lit by red cellophane. There were two boys on the floor and another two squaring up like boxers. There was some broken glass and a chair on its side. Harry pulled at the two on the floor and shouted 'Stop it!' One was Mick, and underneath him the tall leader of the gang. Mick stood up. The tall boy kicked at him. 'It's all right,' Harry said. The tall boy's legs caught him round the ankles and he sat down. Mick came forward. 'No,' Harry said. He and the tall boy stood up. 'You're big, but I'll fight you,' the tall boy said. 'Come outside,' Harry said. 'I'll get you, Mick,' the tall boy said.

Harry took Mick and the tall boy by the arm. The tall boy flung his hand away. Harry went with Mick out to the front lawn, the others following him. Mick said 'I'm sorry, Mr Gates, I heard him call someone a name I don't like.' The tall boy walked round in the darkness and spat. Harry said to him 'Why do you want to come in if you break it up?'

A boy who had not spoken before said 'Lot of coppers' kids, now they're too good for us.' He was a dark good-looking boy wearing a sweater with bars across it. 'How can – ' Harry began. 'We were all at school,' the dark boy said; 'now their parents tell 'em not to mix.' Harry looked at him: 'You're mixing now.' 'They don't like it,' the boy said. 'Well nor do you,' Harry said.

There were dark trees rustling in the sky above. Harry's voice trembled. He said 'Listen, you've got to try, you can't mix if you fight.' They stood in silence. The tall boy came up to Harry and said 'D'you always talk like that?; 'Like what?' Harry said. 'You've got to try,' the tall boy said, putting on an effeminate accent and flouncing with a hand on his hip. Some of the boys began to laugh. Mick said 'Stop that!' and stepped forward. The tall boy jumped on him and they began fighting again. The white-haired boy dragged at a broken post in the fence and got it out of the ground. He turned towards Harry. Harry crouched.

A deep voice just outside the gate said 'Oh now, just a minute!' Jules's head appeared against the night sky. He took hold of the tall boy and said 'You! Carter!' The fighting stopped. Jules put his face close to the tall boy's and said in a quick cockney voice 'Want me to get the boys out, do you, hm?' The white-haired boy put the post down. 'That's better,' Jules said slowly; 'let's all be friends!'

Harry said 'Those who want to come back in, can, the rest go.'

The tall boy and four others went and stood in the road. The dark boy and one other stayed.

Harry said 'Jules! Thank heavens! what made you come?'

'Well me house 'as burned down,' Jules said.

'You're all right?' Harry said. 'You want to stay here?'

'Well – ' Jules said. He scratched his head.

'Of course,' Harry said. 'Come on in.' In the sitting-room, the music had started again. The girls were flicking and spinning with one hand holding their skirts down. Harry said 'who were the boys you threatened 'em with?'

'Oh just friends,' Jules said.

Harry was breathing fast. 'Made them stop quick enough!' He laughed.

'Oh they're feeble!' Jules said.

'I was petrified!' Harry said. He looked round. 'We're having a dance!'

Jules rubbed his hands. 'So I see,' he said. Someone had turned the volume up. The walls of the house shook.

Jerril opened the front door of his house from the street and said to a man who was with him 'Please come in.' The man with the long mournful face said 'Thank you.' 'What did you say your name was?' 'Cartright,' the man said.

Jerril went to the L-shaped studio on the first floor. Annie was reading a book. He said 'This is Mr Cartwright, his house has burned down.' He went past Annie and looked at a piece of iron sculpture by the window.

Cartwright was wearing his black jersey and jeans and a new pair of orange shoes. Annie said 'You've had a fire?'

'Yes,' Cartwright said.

'How terrible. Would you like a drink?'

'Thank you.' He sat down and started undoing his shoes.

'How did it happen?' Annie said.

'Well, you see, I live in a cupboard.' Cartwright's voice became slurred as he struggled with his shoes. 'It's a vewy low went, but an Indian landlord boarded it up. We told him we'd use the board as firewood.'

'And did you?'

'Yes.'

'I do see,' Annie said.

She handed him a whisky. He examined the sole of a foot.

Jerril said to Annie, 'Aren't you drinking?'

Annie's face went flat. She said 'No.'

'The fire bwigade came to put it out,' Cartwright said. 'Evewyfing was all wight before, but now it's soaked.'

'How did you two meet?' Annie said.

'In the pub,' Cartwright said.

Jerril had poured out a glass of whisky and he brought it to Annie and handed it to her. 'Go on,' he said. Annie's face crumpled again as if there were pressure on it in a wind-tunnel. She took the glass.

'These shoes are killing me,' Cartwright said.

Jerril moved round the room. He said in a high-pitched voice 'I saw Lydia this morning, she sent you her love, she says Harry's got a new boy-friend.'

Annie drank some of the whisky. It brought tears to her eyes. She said to Cartwright 'Where will you live?'

'I told him he could stay the night here,' Jerril said. He came and stood by Annie.

'I'm afraid it won't be very comfortable, there's only the sofa,' Annie said.

Jerril put an arm round Annie's waist and pulled her towards him. His eyes were in rectangular slits and his body seemed to vibrate. He kissed her neck. He said 'Very beautiful tonight, hm?'

Cartwright watched them. Annie was pulled over on one leg.

'Very sexy,' Jerril said, 'don't you think so?'

'Yes,' Cartwright said.

Annie said 'I'll make up the sofa.'

'He can come in with us,' Jerril said.

Annie moved away and went out of the room. She went to the bedroom on the top floor which had the one double bed in it. She took her handbag and put some things in it from the dressing-table and picked up her coat. She passed the studio on the way down. Jerril was on the ground floor. He said 'Where are you going?' Annie said 'I told you I would – '

Jerril stretched his arms across the passage. He said 'You're neurotic!'

'Every time that it happens,' Annie said.

'You won't behave like a normal human being!' He suddenly clutched his head. 'Oh – '

Annie waited at the bottom of the stairs. 'I'm not well,' Jerril said. He staggered. He slid to the floor with his legs across the passage.

Annie watched him. His black curly hair and forehead were like the plateau of a mountain, his nose and lips and chin pressed close together.

'Do you want to destroy me?' Jerril said.

Annie stepped over him and went to the front door. After she had gone, Jerril stood up and went into the kitchen. He opened a cupboard and took out some bread and began to eat.

* * *

172

Richard was in his bedroom in his pyjamas watching a portable television set. He held a piece of metal like a truncheon in his hand. There was a burst of tinny music from the television and then letters whirling round before they became legible and a voice said 'Indirect Questions! the *intelligent* parlour game!' A man with long white hair and spectacles sat behind a desk. He said 'Good evening, once again we welcome you. . . .' There was a blast of jazz from the gramophone downstairs. Richard turned the television volume up. '. . . and Lydia Sykes, a newcomer to our faculty.' There was his Aunt Lydia's face absolutely white like a clown's. Richard blushed. He turned the brilliance knob and her face went dark. 'We start with our first *viva voce* and the letter is "M",' the man said. Richard turned another knob and Lydia's forehead stretched enormously and her mouth became squashed into her chin. Richard began to roll about with giggles. 'What flower?' 'Marigold.' 'What composer?' 'Monteverdi,' Lydia said.

Richard heard footsteps on the stairs. He stood up and held the piece of metal like a truncheon behind his back. Helen came in.

She said 'Richard, what are you doing, you should be in bed.'

'It's Aunt Lydia,' Richard said.

There was a tramp of dancers downstairs like an army marching. Helen said 'This dreadful noise.' She went to turn the television off.

'Oh, can I have it on till they go?' Richard said.

Helen looked at him. 'All right,' she said.

'Daddy hasn't been up yet to say prayers.'

'Does he always say prayers?'

'Yes,' Richard said. There was a shout of laughter downstairs.

'They'll be going soon,' Helen said.

'Was there a fight with the Teddy boys?'

'Don't worry,' Helen said.

'Oh I'm not worrying,' Richard said.

Helen went downstairs. The dancers were jerking in the ghostly purple light. Harry was talking to a red-haired boy who had a girl hanging on to his shoulder. The boy was saying 'All this sex, sex – '

Helen said 'Richard wonders if you could say prayers.'

'I will in a minute,' Harry said.

The boy with dark glasses said 'Mr Gates, I'm afraid your neighbour is banging on the wall.'

'Oh bang back at her,' Harry said.

The music changed to a faster beat. Helen noticed that a silver cigarette box was missing from one of the tables. There were a boy and a girl in the corner kissing. All the lights suddenly came on. Helen turned back towards Harry.

Jules was with the girl with piled-up hair. He called out 'Harry, aren't you dancing?' 'I'm too old!' Harry said. 'You weren't that other night!' Jules said. 'Were you dancing the other night, Mr Gates?' the red-haired boy said. 'You should have seen him!' Jules said.

By the gramophone there was a group of girls standing. Harry was watching them. Helen followed where he was looking and saw a tall pretty girl with thin legs and silver-coloured hair. Harry was smiling. Helen turned away. Harry walked across the floor and said to the pretty girl 'Will you dance with me?'

The girl frowned and turned her back on him. The boy with red hair called 'Hard luck, Harry!'

Harry walked back across the floor. He was blushing.

Helen went into the kitchen, where there were glasses with dregs of lemonade in them and plates with crumbs. She began to tidy. The boy with dark glasses came in and said 'Oh hullo, Miss Mason, can I help you?' 'Thank you, Paul,' Helen said. They washed and dried in silence. Then Paul said 'Actually, I don't think tonight was a good idea.' 'Don't you, Paul?' Helen said. 'Well I'm not criticizing Mr Gates, he's been most good to us, but I don't think it's right he should be imposed on.' 'I think he wanted to make friends with those boys,' Helen said. 'But you can't, they only take advantage of it.' 'I hope it didn't spoil your dance,' Helen said. 'Mr Gates is too good to people,' Paul said; 'he doesn't really know what they're like.'

Annie stood on the pavement and looked up at a window in a block of flats two storeys above her. It was closed. She turned to the gutter and found a piece of tin, and threw it. It flew past a policeman just coming round the corner. Annie smiled. She said 'I'm so sorry, I've left my key.'

The policeman looked at her, at the window, at the piece of tin, the way he had come, then went to the front door of the block of flats and pushed on it. 'You've tried the bell?'

'I'm afraid he, I mean they, are very heavy sleepers.'

175

The policeman said 'Married couple?'

'Yes.'

'Got anywhere else to go?'

'I know there's a little window at the back that's open, d'you think I could climb in?' Annie said.

'Can't do that,' the policeman said.

'Oh well, good night,' Annie said. She walked away.

She went by side streets round to the back of the block of flats again. There was an alley-way with dustbins. She reached up to a window which opened horizontally. She put one foot on a dustbin and pushed, getting her head through the window. Then the dustbin fell with a crash. Her knees bumped the wall. A voice behind her said "Ullo, 'ullo 'ullo!'

Annie said 'Maurice, help me.'

'Old Mother *Hubbard*,' Maurice said. 'Coming quietly?'

Annie slipped, scraping her legs. Maurice caught her. He said 'Six *and* out.' He was dressed in a white bathrobe belted at the waist.

Annie sat on a dustbin and groped for her shoes. She said 'Maurice, can I stay here?'

'Tobacco *Road*,' Maurice said.

'I've lost my key,' Annie said. She looked at him. There was a muscle moving in his jaw as if he were chewing. She said 'The key of *my* flat. I only want to sleep on your sofa.'

'Of course,' Maurice said. 'Come on up.'

'You are an angel,' Annie said.

They went in at a back door and up two flights. There was a door in a passage ajar. Inside was a small box-like hall with a kitchen and a bathroom leading off. Beyond it was a bed-sitting room where Jenny was sitting up in bed. She said 'Oh hullo.'

Maurice said 'You do know Jenny, Jenny Wright, Annie, don't you?'

Annie said 'Hullo.' She looked at Jenny with her golden hair and her white nightdress. She said 'I do think – ' then her eyes filled with tears. She sat down. 'I do think you are loyal friends!'

Maurice said 'What about a cup of tea?'

'I'll make some,' Jenny said. She got out of bed and went to the kitchen.

'So cold out,' Annie said. She dabbed at her eyes. 'And so useful of you both to be here. I told a policeman you were a married couple, I don't think he believed me.'

'I thought they'd got you at last,' Maurice said.

'I do think there are extraordinary coincidences,' Annie said. She looked round the room. 'Can I really sleep on your sofa?'

'Yes.'

'I think they all mean something,' Annie said. 'There's a pattern. You don't know it at the time, but you do afterwards.'

Jenny came in carrying cups. Her nightdress had holes in it. Maurice said to her 'Cover yourself up, hm?' and then to Annie 'Go on – '

'I'm just talking,' Annie said.

'Maurice loves a good talk!' Jenny said.

Maurice said 'As a matter of fact we are thinking of getting married.'

'Oh are you?' Annie said. She looked at Jenny. 'I'm so terribly glad!'

Maurice said 'And what about – well – you, hm?'

Annie said 'Jerril's mother and father were killed in Auschwitz, did you know?'

'No,' Jenny said.

'He was in a camp for a time. Then he came to England. He had to be successful. He needs – ' she broke off: ' – a lot!' She laughed. 'Don't we all!' She stood up. She leaned forward and kissed Jenny on the cheek.

'There's the kettle,' Jenny said. She padded out to the kitchen.

'Love,' Annie said. 'What we go through!'

'Look after yourself,' Maurice said.

Harry stood in Father Patterson's bare room with just the bed and table and wash-stand and chair and crucifix. Father Patterson sat on the bed with his head against the wall. Harry said 'I got your letter this morning. I didn't know.'

'But you have seen Jules?' Father Patterson said.

'Yes, he stayed last night with us,' Harry said. 'But I didn't know about his father and mother, and grand-father, and the paper and all that.'

'I thought you might have some ideas,' Father Patterson said.

'Oh yes,' Harry said. He began to pace up and down. 'I know it all, the whole pattern. It's the only thing I do know.'

'You know his family?' Father Patterson said.

'His parents were friends of my parents,' Harry said.

178

His voice began to shake. 'They used to go round the brothels of Marseilles together. My sister Lydia was one of his grandfather's girl friends, when she was just married and he was in the south of France.'

Father Patterson said nothing.

'Oh God!' Harry said. He stretched his eyes dramatically. 'The spiv aristocracy! When you're part of it – a child of it – there's years of it behind you. You love money and live in castles and dream of princesses. It's all unreal. It's foursomes in the brothels of Marseilles, voyeurs and exhibitionists, the modern ways of making love. You can't do anything straight, you can't commit yourself. You pretend, pretend to pretend, to keep yourself safe.'

'What about Jules?' Father Patterson said.

'You're protected,' Harry said, 'there's always another dream to run to. Jules tried to get away but he's only got to his gangs and fighting.'

'What will you tell him?'

'Just to get out,' Harry said. 'And stay out. But I don't know if he will.'

'Why not?'

'Because it's difficult,' Harry said. He sat on the chair and tipped it back. 'It's almost impossible to change.'

Father Patterson's face went long and tired.

'You have to be stretched,' Harry said. 'At your heart. Like the rack.'

Father Patterson grunted.

'You funk it,' Harry said. 'You don't understand. You say – why should it happen to me? I was born like this. And it's true. My sister Lydia – you can't blame her.

Nor my parents. Their parents were useless gentry with beggars at the bottom of their drive. And you love the old life, you cling to it, you're conditioned like a dog.' Harry shook his head. 'There's a world I still love. It's death, but at least not painful.' He tipped the chair so far back that he was almost horizontal. 'You know I'm talking about myself?'

'Yes,' Father Patterson said.

'And then you blame God. You say – why did God fix things like this? And you know the answer – that God doesn't fix things, except for you to be free. But then you say – All right I know, but I can't do it.'

'Why can't you?' Father Patterson said.

'Because – first – you don't know how. You say – how can I be free? And then someone tells you. And you funk it.'

Father Patterson watched him.

'Because of the pain,' Harry said. 'And your lack of courage.'

There was silence. Then Harry said without altering his position 'Annie Longley rang me up the other night.'

'What did she want?' Father Patterson said.

'That night after we'd had dinner at Palomede,' Harry said. 'That was the night Jules rang up as a joke. Well, I went to see Annie. I thought she might be in trouble.' He laughed. 'She told me how awful I was.'

'How?' Father Patterson said.

'Oh, I'm weak, I run away, I'm not responsible. Annie's a tough nut.'

'What did you say?' Father Patterson said.

'What I wanted to say was – what about my good works, my boys, my youth club?'

'Why didn't you?'

'Because even if it were true – ' Harry tipped forward. 'Oh, we had a riot last night. I must tell you.' He leaned back again. 'Because even if it were true, Annie's right.' He waited. 'You think she's right?'

'What do you think?' Father Patterson said.

'Annie's very clever,' Harry said. 'She knows. She's also a sort of – ' he waved an arm ' – there are people like that – a sort of guide, in one's life, in the unconscious.' He balanced with his eyes closed.

'Then why don't you do what she says?'

'What does she say?' Harry said.

Father Patterson said 'I thought she did.'

'I've said, because of fright,' Harry said.

'At what?'

'At the whole world. At breaking your dream. At facing circumstances, heredity, God, instead of blaming circumstances, heredity, God.'

'And what would Annie say about that?'

'That you've got to do it.'

'Then what did she say to you?' Father Patterson said.

Harry was shaking. He said 'Go back to Melissa.'

Father Patterson lifted his hands a few inches off the bed and held them parallel facing inwards on each side. He said 'Have you left Melissa?'

Harry said 'You know what I told you.'

'What?'

'That I was – you know – with Annie that night when

Melissa rang up. When Melissa had a miscarriage. Well, it might not be true.'

'How?' Father Patterson said.

'I mean it was true I was with Annie, but I don't know about the miscarriage.' He screwed his face up. 'It was only beginning. Does one exaggerate guilt?'

Father Patterson said 'No, you confessed it.'

'Yes, but –'

'What matters is now.'

'What is now?' Harry said. He tipped forward and looked round wildly. 'I mean, what is Melissa doing now?'

Father Patterson said 'Well, what is she?'

'Either looking after her father who's ill, or walking out on me because of Annie.'

Father Patterson said 'Which?' He laughed.

'I don't know,' Harry said. He put his head in his hands. 'Does anyone ever know? Melissa and I were so odd. No one understood us. She just left. I *can't* know.'

Father Patterson said 'Why are you and Melissa odd?'

'We're like –' Harry let his breath out with a rush ' – like I said about me and Annie, except that Annie and I were wrong and for a moment, and Melissa and I were right. Melissa knew – knows me. Knows, I mean, how awful. But we were married. Marriage is like that. I had to change. She changed me. You're one flesh.' He looked at Father Patterson. 'A real marriage. You do it or die.'

Father Patterson's face was long with his eyes half-closed.

'Melissa was a New England girl,' Harry said. 'She was all right. Her family were. Well, she told the truth,

I never did. I don't think I knew. None of my family do. Melissa and I loved each other.' Tears came into his eyes. 'She did love me. But something happens in marriage. You know one another. Every minute of the day, no dreams. And things come out of you – not you, not really you – but things fighting each other like your champions. Like knights at a tournament – everything bloody and mean. You want to kill one another.' He put the tips of his fingers together.

'I can't explain, can't remember really. But this happens. Why do marriages break? People fight – they know one another. They haven't got the courage. I once tried to kill myself. I mean, I pretended,' Harry said. 'And Melissa was so calm. Women have a terrible logic. Men have self-pity. Those are their champions.

'Then there was a night when I thought she was going mad. There was a devil – she had been fighting. I hit her. I couldn't stand it. Then she broke. It was worse.

'You can't go on,' Harry said. 'You've got to have a dream.'

Father Patterson said 'Was Annie a dream?'

'For a time,' Harry said. 'Then not.'

'So you couldn't run away?'

'I didn't see her after Melissa rang up. I don't think she wanted to. There'd been too much lying.'

'Isn't there always?'

Harry said 'There might be a dream that would make no demands on you.'

After a silence Father Patterson said 'Then what has changed you?'

'Have I changed?'

183

'Oh yes.'

'Well,' Harry said. He spoke mockingly. 'Melissa – saviour as well as tormentor. Like God.'

'That's only a stage,' Father Patterson said.

'Melissa and I became Christians,' Harry said. 'I once wrote a poem called Manifestations of Divine Love, about how we were being driven round the bend.'

'Would you rather not be free?' Father Patterson said, 'Would you rather it were done for you?'

'Do you know the Christian answer to suffering?' Harry said. 'Suffering – so what!'

'And then do something about it,' Father Patterson said. He looked down at his hands. 'You only say this because you know.'

'What?'

'That it's only hard so long as you're not doing it. It's all right when you are.'

'But what about her?' Harry said. 'She's gone – ' His voice shook so much he could not go on.

'It's yourself,' Father Patterson said.

'I can't.'

'Why not?'

'You don't know what Melissa and I were like,' Harry said. 'I loved her but I hated her.'

'Oh yes yes yes yes yes,' Father Patterson said.

'What do you mean yes yes?' Harry said.

'Of course you hated her,' Father Patterson said. He stood up. He rummaged on his desk for a pipe.

'I mean – ' Harry said.

'You hated her,' Father Patterson said. 'Go on saying

it. That's your so-called champion. Ride him into the ditch, the whole bang lot.'

Harry stared at him.

'You hated her – so what? How can you be loved or loving without also hating it?' He stuffed some tobacco into his pipe. 'Now you come out and fight. Fight your champion.'

Harry said 'It wasn't all me!'

'All you you and Melissa Melissa,' Father Patterson said. 'What is she doing now, have you thought?'

'No,' Harry said.

'Well there you are.'

'I've found it impossible.'

'Knight, armour, lance, chain and ball,' Father Patterson said.

Harry began to laugh. 'I did say I loved her!'

'What did you expect?' Father Patterson said.

Harry groaned.

'You've probably hated God,' Father Patterson said. 'Well, say so.'

Harry rocked backwards and forwards in his chair. He said 'Do you confess things that have helped you?'

'You'll be forgiven,' Father Patterson said.

4

Harry saw below him on the front steps of his house a young man going bald wearing a brown suit and a tie with white fleur-de-lis on it, peering through thick spectacles exactly horizontally like a blind man, saying 'Mr Gates? My name is Ian Arbuthnot, from the *Evening Post*, might I have a few words with you?' His gaze was on a level with Harry's waist. 'Oh yes, come in,' Harry said. The man followed him into the sitting-room holding his shoulders hunched and his head on one side. Harry said 'You spoke to Father Patterson the other day didn't you?' 'You do know Father Patterson then?' the man said. He looked at the seat of the chair carefully before he sat on it. 'I must explain my visit, I'm doing some articles for the *Post* on the subject of social welfare work and I was given your name....' His voice had an indeterminable accent, part Scottish and part Welsh. He pulled a notebook from his pocket. '... so I thought I'd come and see you first.'

'I'm afraid I won't be much help,' Harry said.

'We'll see.' He unexpectedly sounded hostile. He bent over the notebook. 'Now, is it true you work with boys who have been in trouble with the police?'

'I do some work with the probation office,' Harry said.

'Have you an official position, Mr Gates?'

'No. I worked there as a learner while doing a Social Science course, since then I've been unofficial.'

'Unofficial what?'

'Well, keeping an eye on some boys, helping with jobs and that sort of thing.'

The man wrote in his notebook. He said 'So you have no official position at the probation office.'

'No,' Harry said.

'Can you tell me, Mr Gates, what is this Social Science course as you call it?'

'It's a two-year course at London University for social workers,' Harry said.

'And what is the outcome?' The man's pen hung above the notebook. 'I mean, a degree or something?'

'A diploma.'

'You've got it?'

'Yes,' Harry said.

He did not write this down. He blinked.

'I suppose I could get an official job,' Harry said, 'but I don't want one at the moment.' The man seemed not to hear. 'I do some other work tied up with this, with the Help Thy Neighbour Service, a local – '

'Excuse me, Mr Gates, I find it difficult to follow my questions.'

'Sorry,' Harry said.

'These boys, how do you get in touch with them?'

'Well either through this Service, as I was saying, or they come round here.'

'They come to your house?'

'Yes.'

'Socially as well as on business?'

'You could call it that.'

'Would it be true to say you open your doors to these delinquent boys?'

'My friends,' Harry said.

'You call them your friends?'

'Yes,' Harry said.

'They can come in here any hour of the day or night?' Harry did not answer. The man looked straight at him for the first time. His eyes seemed to have had milk spilled over them. 'Does the probation office know you do this work?'

'Of course.'

'I'm only asking.'

'They could come in any hour,' Harry said. 'They don't.'

'Do they stay the night?'

Harry felt frightened. He put his hand to his coat lapel and made an imperceptible sign of the cross.

'Surely they'd sometimes want to?'

'One or two have stayed when there was nothing else, but it's not a good idea,' Harry said.

'Why not?'

'It's difficult to explain,' Harry said. The man was sitting hunched. Harry thought – He is like a child about to cry.

'You mean these boys might get the wrong idea?'

'It's just a problem about not being dependent,' Harry said.

He looked away. There were noises from the kitchen. Helen was talking to a tradesman. Outside, the sky was white. The man said 'Would you say you took up this work as a sort of compensation, to make up to society for a guilt in some way?'

'Oh that's a way of putting it,' Harry said, 'but I don't think true.'

'How do you mean?'

'There's a negative explanation for everything,' Harry said.

'Are you married, Mr Gates?'

'Yes.'

The man blinked. 'Is your wife here?'

'In America.'

'On a visit?'

'She's looking after her father.'

'And when she was here, did she approve of your work?'

'What on earth has this got to do with it?' Harry said.

The man seemed to struggle to find words. He jerked his head. 'I'm interested in personalities, Mr Gates, I thought I might do something of a profile.'

'I don't want a profile.'

'People are interested in personalities. Your background – parents. Are they alive?'

'My mother's dead.'

'And your father?'

'He's secretary to the Monte Carlo Jockey Club.'

The man looked up. 'Is that serious?'

'No.'

'Have you brothers or sisters, Mr Gates?'

189

'A sister. She's married to a man called Sykes.'

'You have a private income?'

'Some.'

The man looked round the room. 'Your wife has money?'

Harry said. 'What do you really want?'

The man swallowed. After a pause he said 'These boys are working-class I suppose, can you give me particulars of one?'

'No,' Harry said.

'I could see him to get his point of view.'

'No,' Harry said.

The man blinked. 'You're being very cautious, Mr Gates.' He turned back a page in his notebook. 'I see here you say about your work being some form of compensation – That's a way of putting it, but I don't think true. What would you say was true?'

'That'd be a long story,' Harry said. He stood up. 'Would you like a cup of tea?'

The man opened and shut his mouth.

Harry went to the door. He said 'How long have you been with the *Post*?'

'About three years.'

'It must be a difficult job.'

'One can't always write what one would like.'

'I'll get the tea,' Harry said. He went out.

There was a tall house with blackened windows and the front door on one hinge. The stairs were wet. Jules was in a front room with clothes and books in piles. He said 'Careful, it's not safe.' Harry stepped over a rolled-up carpet. He said 'You really did have a fire!'

Through the empty windows came packed noises of the street. Cars were in long lines and people on foot dodged between them. Lights came on and the evening sky was a yellowish colour. Harry said 'I hear you want to go to Australia.'

Jules said 'Who told you?'

'Father Patterson,' Harry said.

Jules was sorting out clothes on the floor and putting some into a cardboard box.

'Go to Australia,' Harry said.

'I'm not sure,' Jules said.

'Do what you want,' Harry said.

In the cardboard box there was a shirt, a few socks, some letters, a pair of football boots. Jules said 'I fell I do, but don't. It sounds stupid.'

Harry said 'I know exactly.'

He looked round the room. 'Are these your belongings?'

'I could travel light!' Jules said.

'What stops you, your grandfather?'

'Oh – ' He spoke in his loud voice; 'In a way.'

'You're not scared?'

'No.'

'You think you owe him something?'

Jules scratched his head.

'You owe him nothing,' Harry said.

Outside the crowds were converging on a street that led to the station. They went in a brown mass, shimmering.

'He looked after us when my father, well – and my mother,' Jules said. 'He was good to us.'

'Hop it,' Harry said. 'Catch the next boat.'

'Then he got me this job,' Jules said.

'Does he give you money?'

'No.'

'Look – ' Harry said. He waved at the black walls.

'Oh I know he's mean!' Jules said.

'Why doesn't he want you to go to Australia?'

Jules squatted on his heels.

'I'll tell you,' Harry said. He sat on the edge of a crate with books in it. 'No, why do you think'

'I've been wondering,' Jules said.

'He wants to keep you,' Harry said. 'Under.' He pointed his thumb down.

'I think that's a bit far-fetched,' Jules said.

'Then you explain it.'

The traffic was hooting in the street outside. A thin rain came down. Windscreen wipers went backwards and forwards like fans.

'Listen,' Harry said. 'Everyone's like this. You have to do it on your own.'

'He's a very remarkable man,' Jules said.

'He's a bloody old sod,' Harry said.

Jules moved his foot up and down on a loose floorboard. There was a banging noise from above, and dust floated.

'I can help you with the money,' Harry said.

'You've been very good to me,' Jules said.

'You don't owe me anything!' Harry said.

192

Jules rocked on to all fours above his cardboard box. He said 'I don't know, I really don't.'

In the clear afternoon light Richard could see the back garden from his bedroom window. He was sitting at the table with his cactus and model of the Taj Mahal. In front of him were his piece of metal like a truncheon, a lump of plasticine, a length of fuse, and a box labelled *Mrs Moffat's Invisible Talcum*. He opened the box and poked his finger into a heap of grey gunpowder. There was a metallic sensation on his tongue. He picked up the piece of iron which was a tube open at one end and blocked at the other with putty, poured the gunpowder into it and rammed it tight. He took the fuse, pushed it through the lump of plasticine, and squeezed it into the hollow end of the tube. Then he looked round, holding the bar carefully upright on the table.

Through the window, across the lawn at the far end of the garden, he saw a boy climb over the fence from outside and drop into a flower bed. The boy was out of sight for a moment; then stood up and two more boys appeared over the fence. They waited, half hidden by trees. Then they walked across the lawn.

Still holding the iron tube, Richard went to the landing and called softly 'Helen?' and then 'Daddy?' There was no answer.

He went to the window on the landing which was above the door leading out into the garden. The lawn was empty. He tried to see directly beneath him, but a piece of roof was in the way. There was a sound of scraping on flag-stones.

Richard straightened the fuse of his bomb and felt in his pocket. There was a box of matches. His heart thumped, and he felt dizzy. He went to the banisters at the top of the stairs.

There was a key in the lock of the back door. By bending down with his head near the floor, he could see it.

He began to go down the stairs on tiptoe, keeping his eyes on the lock. He reached the ground floor. The handle turned. He stopped. The door opened and there were the three boys.

The tall boy stared at him. The others stepped back. The tall boy called 'Come in, come in!' He kept his hand on the door. 'Make yourself at 'ome!'

'What d'you want?' Richard said. His voice squeaked.

The tall boy stared at the iron bar in Richard's hand. He said. 'What's that?' He stretched a hand out. He flicked his fingers for the two boys to come up. 'Mr Gates, um?'

'He's out,' Richard said.

''E said to come in,' the tall boy said. They stepped into the passage. Richard backed away. The tall boy held his hand out. 'Give – '

Richard fumbled in his pocket. The tall boy stepped forward and took his arm, Richard jerked and shouted 'Get out!' The boy reached for the bar. Richard swung it and caught the boy on the elbow. The boy swore and doubled up. One of the other boys took hold of Richard's wrists. Richard was red in the face and snarling. The tall boy hit him across the face. He began to fall down, drawing his knees up. He said 'Oh no,' piteously.

*   *   *

Harry sat at the long table in the committee room with the crucifix on the wall and on either side of it pictures of white-haired clergymen in ermine. Around the table were several clergymen and some laymen and one nun. In front of each was a pile of papers which they occasionally shuffled. The Scotchman was standing up and speaking.

'I realize this is an emergency meeting, but I don't see why we shouldn't deal with matters arising from the minutes. As I remember, we were promised a more detailed statement about expenses and results by Mr Gates – the l. s. d., as one might call it, of the Help Thy Neighbour Service – not only Love, Spirit, Devotion; but also pounds, shillings, pence.'

'I thought I gave that,' Harry said.

The large bald priest in the chair beneath the crucifix said 'This is a special meeting to deal with the winding up of the Service owing to the illness of Father Wodehouse, I don't think we need do much normal business.'

The man with the old Etonian tie said 'As I understand it we're handing over the telephone number and what for once might rightly be called the good will' (he paused for a laugh) 'to this organization in the City.'

'Surely all the more reason for a statement,' the Scotchman said.

Harry stood up and said 'I'm sure I did give a statement about expenses, but if you want something about results, it's almost impossible. I should guess about half the people who've come to us we've helped in obvious ways, a third we hope we have, and there have been some of course who are a farce.'

The Scotchman said 'That is scarcely a statistical picture.'

Harry said 'What are the statistics of crucifixion?' He sat down.

The Scotchman stood up slowly and said 'The point I am trying to make, and I'm sorry if my powers of exposition are not of the strongest, is just that if there had been a little more organization in this business, then perhaps we should not have had this unfortunate breakdown.'

The bald priest said quickly 'We needn't go into that.'

Harry stood up and said 'I think we should, we all know Father Wodehouse has had a breakdown, and it's just because he tried so hard to help so many people that he did. How can you have an effect without the cost of it?' He sat down. The bald priest began to speak. Harry jumped up again: 'I think this must be said, we all shelter behind these committees, and they excuse us from doing anything, and then we are critical of people who do and get hurt.' He sat down.

The Scotchman spread his hands out and said 'May I humbly say I was only talking about the accounts?'

A man with a round face and spectacles said 'I think we should pay careful attention to Mr Macfarlane, his father was one of our founder members and his cousin Prebendary Macfarlane for many years chairman of our Patronage Committee.'

The Scotchman said 'Thank you.'

The bald priest began 'Well perhaps we can now – '

Harry said 'If there's anything wrong with the money I'll make it up.'

The Scotchman said 'Some of us are not so fortunate.'
The nun said in a bell-like voice 'Shame!'
The bald priest went on ' – deal with the agenda.'

Jules went through swing doors with *Staff Only* written
on them and into a passage that smelt of steam and food.
There was a partition down one side with windows that
looked into a kitchen with stainless steel stoves with
ventilators like lights above billiard tables. There were
about twenty men and boys in white smocks and chefs'
hats. Jules tapped on the window. Mick Jackson saw
him and came up wiping his hands. Jules pointed. They
went out through the swing doors to the street.

Jules said 'Mr Gates 'ad something lifted from 'is
room the other night, know about it?' 'What d'you
want?' Mick said. Jules spread his hands out: 'Mr
Gates's been good to us!' 'What was it?' Mick said. 'A
cigarette box,' Jules said. Mick scowled. 'Know where I
can find Ken Carter?' Jules said. Mick looked up the
street as if they might be watched. 'I've not seen you!'
Jules said. 'Try the Albemarle Club,' Mick said. He slid
through the doors like a detective.

There was a policeman about a hundred yards from
the Albermarle Club entrance which had an awning
projecting above it. He was gazing at a wall of advertisement hoardings in bright colours. Three boys went past
him at a run, one of them holding his elbow. They
slowed as they approached the club entrance. On the
opposite pavement there was a boy with orange hair
coming from the other direction. This boy called to
them. The advertisement that the policeman was look-

ing at was of a girl lying on her back with her knees up and a record-player floating in the air just above her. The boy with orange hair crossed the road and the four of them were talking outside the club. The policeman saw the boy holding his elbow spin round and seem to be doing a kind of dance, with a leg lifted. A horse and cart came up the road and blocked his view. There was a puff of steam behind the advertising hoardings. The boy was now lying on the ground and the three others were lurching and pulling at each other's arms like children. The policeman started walking towards them. A flock of pigeons landed and pecked in the wake of the horse and cart. The boy on the ground had risen and was waving an arm at the boy with orange hair like someone throwing a quoit. The others backed away. Then they saw the policeman. They ran, calling the other two. The policeman crossed the road. There was dung in the street which the pigeons pecked at. The two boys had fallen; they were fighting. The boy with the orange hair was on top of the other, who was jerking his head and spitting. 'Now then,' the policeman said. A few yards away there was a knife with blood on it. The policeman pulled a whistle out of his pocket. The boy with orange hair stood up. The boy on the ground seemed to be having a fit: he waved his legs in the air with tight black trousers of a crumbling, soft material, above which his skin was curiously white. The boy with orange hair scratched his head. 'Ah –,' he said, like a groan.

Harry came out of the underground station into the

busy street with low shops and advertisement-boards on top of them like lids. He bought a copy of the *Evening Post*. On the front page there was a picture of a man with a coat over his head being held by two policemen and underneath it a headline *Regent's Park: Arrest*. Harry thumbed through the pages and saw an inside headline *Comforts for* . . . and went past it; then noticed his name. He read –

COMFORTS FOR THUGS
*Ian James takes a look at a sidelight
of the Young Thugs campaign*

I'm a comfort-loving man myself. Also, I like lending a helping hand. But in the problem of teenage crime, who are most in need – the young thugs or their victims?

I heard of an interesting experiment the other day. I went to see Mr Harry Gates, who keeps an open house in North London for boys who have been in trouble with the police. In Mr Gates's comfortable Regency home (3 bed, 2 recep., large garden, rates £100 a year) he told me 'These boys are my friends. They can come in at any hour of the day or night.'

Mr Gates is married, but his wife is in America. Mr Gates lives on his own. Often, he puts boys up for the night. 'I have no official position,' he says 'and I do not want one.'

Why does Mr Gates choose this work? 'Perhaps it is some sort of compensation,' he says.

All right, Mr Gates. But must other citizens suffer?

I spoke to Mr Gates's next-door neighbour, Mrs Kay Simpson, a clothes consultant. She said 'I am afraid to go to sleep at night. These boys are of all varieties. The other night there was revelry till the early hours.'

What do the boys learn from these luxurious surroundings? Will this not lead to more crime, rather than decrease it?

I don't know about you, but I think it is time we stopped handing over our young criminals to the do-gooders – the people who would abolish corporal punishment, the death penalty, and the homosexuality laws.

Should we not ask – *what are their real motives*?

Harry said 'Oh hell.' He looked for somewhere to sit down. There was a square with railings round it. The gate into the garden was locked. He said 'I'm a bloody fool.'

He walked towards his home. He went up the front steps and into the hall and stopped there. He called 'Helen?' The house was quiet. He sat on a chair and stared at the wall. There was a wallpaper of white urns on a grey background. He and Melissa had chosen it together. There had been a shop with huge rolls like lavatory paper, and young men with wavy hair.

He looked down and saw on the floor a grey dust like gunpowder. Beside it was a lump of plasticine with a wire stuck through it. The wall above was slightly scratched. He said 'Richard?' He went to the foot of the stairs and listened, and called again 'Richard?' There was a faint sound like someone singing. He went upstairs and stood outside Richard's door. He said 'Richard?'

He pushed against the door and found it blocked by something drawn up inside. He put a hand round and felt the chest of drawers. He pushed so that the chest scraped back, and squeezed in. Richard was lying on his face on the bed. He made a wailing noise. Harry sat and put a hand on Richard's shoulder and said 'What is it?' Richard pulled the cover of the bed over his head. Harry said 'Is it your chemicals?' The back of Richard's neck was fragile like a bird's. 'It doesn't matter,' Harry said; 'you must tell me.' He tried to pull Richard's head round but Richard snarled and went stiff. 'Darling Richard, what is it then?' Harry held him; his hair was like wheat. 'Nothing,' Richard cried. Harry thought O, God help us, God help us. 'They came in here,' Richard said. 'Who?' Harry said. 'They hit me!' Richard screamed. Harry said in terror 'It's all right, did they hurt you?' He thought – I'm not going to be able to bear this. He felt Richard's arms, legs, body. Richard pulled himself away. Harry said 'Where did they hit you?' Richard lay on his face again. Harry said 'Richard, I love you.' Richard said 'Leave me alone, can't you?'

There was a ping like a violin string and a red light went on on Lord Sidney's desk. He shouted 'What is it?' The voice of his secretary said 'Ian Arbuthnot is asking to see you Lord Sidney.' 'What does he want?' 'He says it's most urgent, Lord Sidney.'

When Ian Arbuthnot came in he found Lord Sidney behind his desk with a sheaf of notes in one hand and the other holding his coat lapel. Ian Arbuthnot approached with his gaze unblinking, at the top of Lord Sidney's head. Lord Sidney shouted 'I've got my speech to do!' Ian Arbuthnot said 'I'm sorry, Lord Sidney, but your grandson Cavendish has been arrested.'

Lord Sidney put his notes down and swung himself into profile. He said 'What for?'

'Fighting in the street,' Ian Arbuthnot said.

'Anyone hurt?'

'The other boy.'

'Have the other papers got it?'

'Yes.'

'I see,' Lord Sidney said. He picked up a paper-knife and gripped it. 'Obviously no coincidence.' Ian Arbuthnot stared at him through thick spectacles.

'They haven't wasted much time!' Lord Sidney shouted.

'It couldn't very well. . . .' Ian Arbuthnot began.

'A reprisal!' Lord Sidney shouted. 'I know these people!' He stood up and flexed his shoulders like a boxer. 'I've exposed Gates!'

'I don't think–,' Ian Arbuthnot began again.

'What?' Lord Sidney shouted. He took a cigar. He turned to Ian Arbuthnot and flashed his smile. 'They know my campaign for harsher treatment for young offenders.'

Ian Arbuthnot said nothing. Lord Sidney's eyes had gone like milk. His lips sucked the cigar in an almost perfect 'O'.

'I warned him!' Lord Sidney said. 'Now the consequence!' He lifted his chin like a general taking a salute.

'He's at South Paddington,' Ian Arbuthnot said.

Lord Sidney said 'They won't get me this way.'

'About your grandson,' Ian Arbuthnot said. He took out his notebook. 'What shall I do?'

'Get the lawyer in the morning,' Lord Sidney said.

'And tonight?'

'Nothing,' Lord Sidney said. He sucked on his cigar..

Ian Arbuthnot's pen hovered over his notebook. He blinked. Lord Sidney walked up and down. He said 'They have immense power. In government, in the church. Degenerates and homosexuals!' His smile went on and off. 'One might say I had a persecution complex were there not such overwhelming evidence.'

Ian Arbuthnot stared at his hands.

'This has happened before,' Lord Sidney said. 'In the Spanish war, my son, a brilliant young man with a fine brain. They said he was with the reds.' Lord Sidney leaned forward. 'Quite untrue. He was a war correspondent.'

Ian Arbuthnot closed his notebook and put his pen in his breast pocket.

'I have to protect myself,' Lord Sidney said. 'My position is too important. No preferential treatment for Cavendish!'

Ian Arbuthnot stood up to go.

'Tell my secretary he won't be at dinner. Tonight of all nights!' Lord Sidney shouted.

The big bald priest sat in Father Patterson's room and puffed a pipe. He said 'Pity you weren't there this afternoon, we had Macfarlane as usual.' He frowned deeply. 'But what about Gates, is he right for the job?'

'I think so,' Father Patterson said. 'He might not be.'

'He let fly this afternoon,' the bald priest said, 'about how useless we were.'

'He's not good at committees.'

'Then he shouldn't be on one,' the bald priest said. He pulled from his pocket a torn-off page of a newspaper and passed it to Father Patterson. 'Have you seen this?'

Father Patterson read it. 'Oh well well well!' he said.

'The press is of the devil,' the bald priest said.

'At least he's not homosexual,' Father Patterson said.

'Oh dear no!' The bald priest puffed.

'But he is away from his wife.' Father Patterson passed the newspaper back. 'That leaves him open I suppose.'

'I don't really understand Gates,' the bald priest said.

Father Patterson said 'Having been brought this far, I can't believe he won't go on.'

'Oh I'm sure,' the bald priest said.

'Also, people like that have a curious power. Something spreads – ' Father Patterson curved a hand outwards ' – even when they're a bit off the rails.'

'Gates was mentioned for this new welfare job,' the bald priest said.

'I don't know,' Father Patterson said.

'He'll go back to his wife?'

'I hope to see him soon,' Father Patterson said.

The bald priest banged at his pipe. 'Well I'll leave it to you. It's true Macfarlane's a menace. Have you heard Wodehouse's remark about him?'

'No.'

The bald priest put on a face and spoke in an ancient, high-pitched voice. 'If Macfarlane had been at the Last Supper, he'd have enquired who had done the catering.' He shook with laughter. Father Patterson stared at him.

'That's very good,' Father Patterson said. 'Have you heard Wodehouse's one about our new bishop?'

'No,' the bald priest said.

Father Patterson assumed the same squeaky, high-pitched voice. 'Like a certain undergarment, uplift guaranteed.' The bald priest stared at him.

'That's very good,' he said.

A bell rang downstairs. They stood up. 'Won't you stay for Evensong?' Father Patterson said.

'If you get through it quickly.'

'Oh we're very civilized,' Father Patterson said. He made way for the bald priest to go out of the door. They both seemed suddenly embarrassed.

Jenny sat in the armchair of Harry's sitting-room. Her legs were drawn up so that the length of her thigh was visible. Her hair went down past one eye and the tip of her nose. She said 'I did love those two days.' 'So did I,' Harry said. 'I have missed you,' Jenny said. Harry floated around her like a bird.

'What have you been doing?' Jenny said.

'We had a fight with some boys here the other day, Richard got mixed up,' Harry said.

'I do think you're brave,' Jenny said. 'You make me feel brave.'

'It's awful for Richard,' Harry said. 'I've taken him to my sister's.'

'You're like a knight,' Jenny said, 'rescuing people.'

'I feel like in the war,' Harry said. He went to the fireplace and leaned above it. There was a coal fire. The room was hot. The curtains were drawn and the lights were on. Jenny's glass had silver bubbles in it; her mouth made it misty as she breathed. Harry said 'I was once taken prisoner. For a few minutes, while fighting went on. I had to escape. I did. I hid behind a tree. A man came after me.'

'I don't remember the war,' Jenny said.

'Everything waited,' Harry said. 'There was snow. I remember the snowflakes.'

'I was a child,' Jenny said.

'He was killed,' Harry said 'just in front of me.' Harry came and sat on the arm of Jenny's chair. Jenny put her head back. He said 'I had to see you.'

'When I was a child I heard my mother was in a lunatic asylum, did I tell you?' Jenny said.

'Yes,' Harry said.

'I used to go there.'

'Is your mother still alive?'

'I sometimes see her,' Jenny said.

Harry moved away. On the mantelpiece there was a card which said 1001 YEARS OF ARABIAN ART. He stared at it. He said 'Are you all right with Maurice?'

'I'm like his child,' Jenny said. 'But I look after him.'

'Maurice is kind,' Harry said.

Jenny said 'Did you know Jerril was in a camp?'

'No, was he?' Harry moved round the room. He said 'Perhaps Annie – '

'What?'

'We all come up against our brick walls,' Harry said.

Jenny said 'Harry, did you go to church that morning?'

Harry said 'Which morning?' and then laughed. 'No, but I could have.'

Jenny said 'I don't see how you could.'

Harry knelt in front of her. 'Oh that's how it works. Look, look – ' he pulled her head down. 'You make me brave!'

'Why?' Jenny said. There were tears in her eyes.

'It does work,' Harry said. 'It's true. I do love you!'

'I'm so glad you rang up,' Jenny said. 'Let's go and have dinner!'

'Yes,' Harry said. He jumped up.

'Where shall we go?'

'Japan,' Harry said. 'They are always arranging flowers in Japan.'

'Singing tirra lirra by the river,' Jenny said. She felt for her shoes. 'Would you like to go to Palomede?'

'The first place I saw you!' Harry said.

Jenny went to a looking-glass and stood on tiptoe. She took from her bag a broken-off paint brush and drew two black lines curving upwards from her eyes. She said 'Maurice said he might be there.'

'Good,' Harry said.

They went down the front steps and through the garden. Jenny looked up at him. She said 'I do love you too, you know!'

* * *

Lydia Sykes sat in a corner of the Rolls Royce wrapped in soft white furs and with a gold bandeau round her forehead. Her face was white and unwrinkled and startlingly beautiful. In the other corner Lord Sykes was in evening dress. Lydia said 'If I have to shake hands with that dreadful old man, I'll crack his knuckles.'

Lord Sykes said 'He can't have known about Harry.'

The car drew up at the entrance to a large hotel. There was an awning from the road to the door, and a man in brown striped livery. Lydia climbed out holding her skirt above her ankles. A small crowd murmured. Lydia's eyes suddenly filled with tears. She went up the carpeted steps stooping.

In a room with red-and-white velvet wallpaper Lord Sidney took the hand of each of his guests as they approached and did his smile like a lighthouse blinking on and off. He wore a red silk sash diagonally across his chest with an elaborate medallion in the middle. Lydia held her hand out and Lord Sidney bent over it and said huskily 'Lydia!' Two enormous tears had formed at the bottom of her eyes; and at the moment when Lord Sidney looked up they fell, like raindrops, one after the other down her cheeks. She drew her hand away. Lord Sidney gazed after her. Lord Sykes took his hand that was still limp, and said 'Forty years behind the mast, what?'

'What?' Lord Sidney said.

Lydia went through the red-and-white room with her gold bandeau forward like a Shakespearian soldier. People made way. She went through double doors and entered a banqueting room with one long table at the head and smaller tables scattered beyond it. There were waiters standing about with napkins Lydia cried 'Oh Luigi, where am I?'

A small fat man in a dinner-jacket came towards her through the tables cornering like a racing motorist. He took her hand as it went past him and bowed over it briefly as if changing gear. 'I know I'm somewhere!' Lydia said. She moved along the top table looking at the cards with names. 'And I'm not sitting next to –' she pounced on a card and moved off down the room with the head waiter trying to overtake her ' – that dreadful old man!'

They came to a stop. The other waiters flicked their napkins. The two tears were still like pearls on Lydia's cheeks. She said 'Oh where shall I go?'

The head waiter drew a huge sheet of paper from under his arm. He said 'Mr Byng, my lady?'

'Luigi!' Lydia cried.

'Mrs Poole?' the head waiter said.

'Emma Poole? Is Peter here?' Lydia followed the head waiter to a table for four. 'And, Leo!' she said. She put her hand on her heart. 'And Annie Longley! Luigi, be an angel, and change me with Mrs Poole. You know she'd love it!'

'My lady,' the head waiter said.

Lydia moved off again towards the red-and-white room. She cried 'I'll never forget you!' The tears had disappeared from her cheeks.

Lord Sidney saw Lord Sykes talking to a dark-haired girl at the bar. He recognized Annie Longley. She had long brown arms, a white dress up to her throat. He made his way towards them. Emma Poole appeared in his path wearing a ginger wig. Lord Sidney altered course and found himself by Pansy Dooland, who kissed him on the cheek. Emma Poole was coming after him but was caught by the head waiter who gesticulated at her with an enormous sheet of paper. Lord Sidney looked for Lydia. A man in crimson livery flung open the doors and bellowed 'My lords, ladies and – ' In the hush, there was a familiar wail sounding like 'ee-o!' Lord Sidney saw Lydia embracing a short dark man like a frog. 'Served!' bellowed the crimson man.

When they were seated, Lord Sidney found himself next to Emma Poole. He leaned towards Lord Sykes, four places on his other side. He shouted 'Where's Lydia?'

.'Upset,' Lord Sykes said.

'What about?'

'Her brother Harry,' Lord Sykes said. His blue eyes wrinkled.

'It's been such a long time. . . .' Emma Poole said to Lord Sidney. Steam from soup drifted up past his face.

'Harry who?' Lord Sidney shouted.

'Gates,' Lord Sykes said. 'And the *Post*.' The three people between them sipped their soup.

From a table at the far end of the room there was a shout of laughter. People at the top table stretched their necks. Lord Sidney stared at the ceiling.

At the table for four, Lydia sat between Peter Poole and Leo Johnson. Annie was opposite. She said 'Sid would have been a bugger if he'd been at a public school.'

'Have I told you about him and my mother?' Peter Poole said. 'Well, when he first got rich, just after the first war, he invited my mother to dinner, and she found herself *à deux* in a little room like a Moorish bath. Well, when she opened her napkin, a diamond bracelet fell out into the soup, and she picked it out and said "You must tell your cook about this."'

Lydia did another peal of laughter and crammed her napkin against her mouth. She looked round the table with wide, childish eyes.

'Do you know how he made his first hundred thousand?' Leo Johnson said. 'He got the french-letter contract for Ireland.'

They rolled about with laughter. Lydia put her head on the table.

At the top table Emma Poole opened a programme with a coat of arms on the outside and read

A dinner to
LORD SIDNEY PC
given by his many devoted friends
in gratitude for a lifetime of public service
on the occasion of the 40th anniversary of the
founding of the Sidney Press.

Lord Sidney beckoned to a waiter. He said 'Send my secretary.' He cleared a space in front of him. He tore a page from his programme and began writing on it.

At the table for four Lydia said 'Do you know the real thing about him? His secret?'

'Do tell,' Peter Poole said.

'You mean, Madeleine?' Leo Johnson said.

'Oh, Leo!'

'Madeleine who?' Peter Poole said.

'His daughter-in-law,' Annie said.

'He had an affair with her,' Leo Johnson said.

'But you don't know, you don't know!' Lydia said.

'Oh what?' Peter Poole said.

'They had a child!' Lydia said. 'Sid had to keep him from the light of day!'

'Like Glamis,' Leo Johnson said.

'Who do you think Glamis was?' Peter Poole said.

'Oh I shouldn't have said that!' Lydia said.

'Not was, is,' Leo Johnson said.

'One of your patients?' Annie said.

'Oh I shouldn't!' Lydia said. 'I made it up!'

Lord Sidney had stopped eating. He held his hand below the jewelled medallion on his heart. There was a bad pain in his side. The room was blurred to him. In his waistcoat-pocket he felt the monocle he never wore in public.

The noise and heat increased. People laughed and spoke to him. He took sips of iced water and felt in another pocket for his cigars. He had boxes of these sent each month from Havana. He had once been to the factory where they were made: girls with strong fingers had flicked among brown leaves, pressing them.

The crimson man banged on the table and bellowed 'My lords, ladies and – ' Lord Sidney felt his cigar. It was smooth like something living. 'Pray silence for – ' He put it in his lips, and sucked.

Through a cloud of smoke he heard Benjamin Sykes speaking: '... gathered here tonight for one who is to all of us...' Lord Sidney screwed up one eye to try to see where Lydia was sitting. He had once been in love with Lydia. '... one of the truest and most loyal, in hardship or calm waters...' He had given her a diamond necklace and had hung it round her neck. She had stayed the night with him at Cap Ferrat, among the mimosa and smell of jasmine.

At the table for four they had torn strips off their programmes and were playing a writing game. Peter Poole had passed to Lydia his piece of paper, which said

> Lord Sid, descended from the ape

Lydia bent over it. She added

> Retains his old ancestral shape
> Oh! what mortal hand or eye

She folded over the first two lines and passed the paper to Dr Johnson, with just the last line showing. He turned it this way and that as if it were an ink blot.

There was a burst of clapping. The crimson man bellowed again. Lord Sidney stood up. He gazed into space, smiling.

A waiter was moving between the tables. He came to Lydia and handed her a huge orchid. It was flame-coloured, streaked with pink. Lydia put her hand on her heart. With the orchid there was a page torn from a programme which said

All shall be atoned for
You have the happiness of my anniversary in your hands
Forgive the ignorance of a foolish but a fond old man.

Two huge tears formed at the bottom of Lydia's eyes.

'My friends!' Lord Sidney shouted. He flung his arms out.

Jerril Muller stood on the top landing of the house where there was no carpet. He held a coil of rope like a clothes line. He had taken off his shirt, vest and shoes, and was looking at a skylight. The frame was fastened by a rack and pinion. Between this and the jamb of the skylight there was a gap crossed at the bottom by the bolts holding the pinion wheel.

He went into the lumber room at the front of the house where there were trunks and the plaster statue and cases of stuffed birds. He took a chair and dragged it to the landing and climbed on it. Stretching on tiptoe, he put the end of the rope through the gap above the iron bolts and pulled it down and tied a loop in it with a slip knot.

He put his head through the noose and tightened it. Taking up the slack on the rope by pulling at the free end he swayed forwards, with half his weight on his throat. He hung like this with his eyes closed till the muscles of his legs trembled.

He pulled himself upright and took the noose off and stepped down. He went to the studio on the first floor and undressed. There was a large plate of splintered glass on the ground. He knelt by it.

Pink and gold strands spread beneath the surface. He took a pointed instrument and prised up a triangle of glass, leaving raised edges. He did this at several places. Then he stretched his arms over the surface and crawled on it. The glass was cold.

He elongated himself and lay down with his arms above his head. As he breathed the patch in front of his mouth became misty. There was a sensation of fire down his body. He moved, feeling the glass cut him.

Beyond the patch of mist, in front of his eyes, was a raised piece of glass like a mountain. He covered it with his wrist. He pressed. Blood ran from beneath his hand. He felt a violent thirst. He was in a valley, buried. He struggled. There were nails through him.

He knelt up and looked at the glass underneath. It was smeared with blood round the raised patches like volcanoes. His body was patched with blood. He held the gash in his wrist over a hole in the glass and the blood dripped into it. It thickened there.

He stood up. He went upstairs into the bedroom and lay down on the bed. He picked up a magazine. He read

The urgent issues which confront the Labour movement concern the traditional link between the party and the unions. This has in the past prevented them from becoming no more than sectional pressure groups without affiliations.

He put the magazine down. He lay looking at the ceiling. He stretched up a hand with the wrist horizontal and turned it this way and that. He yawned. Swinging himself up, he sat on the edge of the bed with his arms on his knees and his head down. His wrist had stopped bleeding. He turned his toes inwards and screwed them up.

He went and stood on the chair on the landing again and put his head through the noose. He pulled the free end of the rope tight and fastened it round his waist. He leaned with his weight on the ropes and there was a sensation as if he were being cut in pieces. He put his arms up and held on to the ropes above him and swung his feet off the chair so that he was hanging. He stretched a foot to rest it on the chair again but he hit the chair, knocking it over. He groped. The pressure on his throat and waist increased as if something were being born in him. There was darkness and light together. He began to loosen his hold on the ropes above him. He flung his arms out so that he was floating for a moment like a bird above flames.

The telephone rang in the dark and Harry picked up the receiver. Annie's voice said 'Hullo-o,' copying his. Then – 'Are you alone? Can I talk? I've been having dinner with your sister Lydia.'

Harry switched on the light and looked at his watch. It was after midnight. He lay back in bed. 'I'm rather drunk,' Annie said. 'We had such an evening! There was a dinner for Lord Sidney, such disgusting food, we were with Leo Johnson and Peter Poole, do you know? Leo told us stories about his patients, he had Lord Sidney once, for hysterical paralysis of the chest – ' her laugh rang out and echoed in his ear ' – like a feeding mother, don't you think that's apt?' There was a pause. Annie said 'Are you there?'

'Yes,' Harry said.

'Ye-es,' Annie copied him. 'Poor darling, I've rung you in the middle of the night!'

'Where are you?' Harry said.

'In a call box.'

'What are you doing?'

'Oh nothing,' Annie said. 'There's a party at Lord Sid's house, shall I go?'

'What will it be like?' Harry said.

'Oh miles above Park Lane, and everyone longing to throw themselves out. Your sister and brother-in-law and all your old friends.'

'Shall I come?'

'And catch us, darling?' Annie's voice lilted. 'Everyone who's so beastly to you? Did you mind that article in the *Post*?'

'Not much,' Harry said.

'So good for you,' Annie said. 'Have you been sacked yet from your work?'

'I'm being considered for a higher post,' Harry said.

Annie's laugh rang out. 'How Freudian!'

'The woman next door has boarded up her letter-box as protection,' Harry said.

Annie's voice went solemn. 'Oh, darling! Now that is serious. You will be careful?'

Harry said 'I must tell you, there's a man called Bill who often comes round to us for money, and we all thought he must be the Regent's Park murderer. Then on the day the murderer was arrested, Bill fell down a manhole and cricked his neck, don't you think that's synchronicity?'

Annie said 'Oh darling, it is nice talking to you!'

'And so we go on,' Harry said.

'Will you come to the party?'

'I don't think so.'

'I'd like to introduce you to Sid.'

'I'd say – didn't we meet centuries ago, at Monte Carlo?'

Annie said in a far-away voice 'We must get rid of the non-valid symbols.'

'What shall we do with the valid ones?' Harry said.

'Darling, shall I tell you?' Annie's laugh was so loud that Harry held the receiver away from his ear.

He turned on his side and drew his knees up. He switched off the light. He said 'Well, give them my love.'

'I'll go home,' Annie said.

'We'll all go home,' Harry said.

'I've given up my flat,' Annie said.

'Where do you live?'

'Poor Annie's a-cold.'

'You're lucky to be drunk,' Harry said.

The stillness seemed suddenly alive. There was a line between them round the world.

Annie said 'Well there we are.'

'Happy as can be,' Harry said.

'Goodbye.'

'Goodbye, darling.'

'Bless you,' Annie said.

*   *   *

Jules had a dream. He dreamed he was in a police station. There was a room with a counter down the middle behind which a sergeant sat at a telephone switchboard. Jules was on a bench in the opposite half of the room. He had the sensation of being handcuffed; yet when he looked down his wrists were free.

His grandfather came in. He was dressed in a double-breasted overcoat and grey trilby hat like a Chicago gangster of the 1920's. His face was young and puffy with a thin black moustache. He said 'There's no need for explanations.' He held his hand inside his coat like Napoleon. He said to the sergeant 'The usual sentence is seven years.'

Jules had something very important to say, but when he tried he could not make his mouth work. He struggled and said 'You're afraid of dying!' His grandfather changed and became like the last time Jules had seen him – old and with his eyes gone smoky. He had his coat off and his sleeves rolled up and his shirt was open at the neck.

Jules was being marched along a passage between two policemen. They came out on the tow-path of a river. It was night, in the middle of a city. There were iron rings in the stone embankment a few feet above the water. There was the arch of a bridge in deep shadow. One policeman went in front and one behind. In the darkness Jules threw himself sideways towards the water but he hung in the air as if tied to the tow-path. He made swimming movements with his arms while the policeman reached for him. Then he was underneath the water, swimming.

The water became silvery and there were fishes close to his eyes. He came upon the wreck of a ship with a high prow and a curved hole for the anchor chain. Beneath it (or beyond it; he was inside now, finding he could breathe) there were decks and cabins of polished wood. Behind a door there was something trapped. He pulled on the door but could get no leverage; he floated away when he pushed. By an enormous effort he moved the door a few inches and there was the dark edge of a coat like someone drowned. He grasped it and it came towards him and then he could breathe no longer and he had to get to the surface. He kicked, holding the body. He had no strength.

He was on a beach of golden sand with the waves coming in in long white lines. Beyond him there was a group of people standing over a body on the sand. He went over and saw a child with golden hair. The child was wearing a white open-necked shirt. Jules bent over him. A woman's hand stretched out and touched him and rolled him over. It was as if the woman's hand was touching Jules. Jules saw the child's face beneath him; then his own face was looking up at the woman who touched him. He had a sensation of light; as if he were being lifted.

At dawn there was a pink glow over the roofs of the city. The dome of St Paul's appeared magnified like a misplaced lid. A newspaper van came down Fleet Street and bumped into the distance. Perspectives were fore-shortened, making movement appear vertical.

In an all-night café there were yellow neon lights and

yellow-topped tables in a raised circle like a small arena. The man with a long mournful face sat drinking coffee. He wore his black jersey and jeans and bright orange shoes. Opposite him a man was reading a morning paper. There was a huge headline DISASTER: FULL STORY. Beneath it, blurred, a picture of rubble stretched over the whole front page.

On the back page a headline said *Nap goes on Petronella*. Below the paper there was an ashtray with the word CHURCH on its rim in plastic letters. The stub of a cigarette burned in it with a dry smell. The story on the front page began *And there was darkness over the land*. A silver coffee-machine gave a squirt of steam and water. At the yellow tables men sat unshaven and ghostly.

The pink light of the dawn had spread down the fronts of grey stone buildings and was reflected in glass and marble. A pediment with a winged horse shone in flames. The man with the mournful face read *The first peace-time holocaust: thousands feared dead*. He scooped sugar into his coffee-cup and the spoon remained brown-encrusted. He looked outside, where the pink light had appeared on the pavement which seemed to run with it.

He said 'Good God!' The other people in the café had not noticed. The paper had been folded so that the back page hung upside down over the front. By lowering his head he could see a corner of the front page which read *the extent of the tragedy is not* and underneath this *an accident or momentary loss of control*. He edged along the table to the café window. A van came out from beneath an arch with an advertisement diagonally across it saying just PANSY DOOLAND.

He went into the street. A flock of birds rushed past him and disappeared. Far away there were indistinguishable cries. He looked at the silver-blue sky which was like a skin and almost within reach. From behind came the clang of a bell. The streets were empty. He turned down towards the river.

The distance in front of him did not seem to be getting any shorter. The embankment suddenly appeared above the surface of the river. The cries behind him were of birds. The water ran with pink, and seemed on fire. A wind blew and ruffled the paper that lay on benches. The paper was curved over bodies. The bodies were faceless. Looking down the river, towards the east, he saw the sun.

Harry came into Lydia's bedroom. The bed with the canopy above it was littered with letters and morning papers. Lydia held the telephone to her ear. Harry stood by Jerril's picture of pink and yellow glass. Lydia said 'You've been so kind!' She put the receiver down.

'What haven't I done!' she said to Harry.

She put a pair of horn-rimmed spectacles on her nose.

'The ambassador's doing your visa, you go round and ask for – ' She wrote something down. 'Your tickets are ready, and money, have you got money?'

'I've embezzled my funds,' Harry said.

'The plane leaves – ' Lydia shuffled through the papers. ''Why all this rush? Where've you been all morning?'

'With Father Patterson,' Harry said.

'Why?'

Harry leaned against the bed and stared at her.

'I don't know why you're so cheerful,' Lydia said. 'Do you know where Melissa is? Have you heard from her?'

'No,' Harry said. Lydia's toes stuck up in a small mound. He waggled them.

'You make me so mad!' Lydia said.

'Can it be,' Harry said 'that out of the length of the world we will not find one another?'

'Have you seen the papers?'

'Oh yes,' Harry said. He began walking up and down. 'There's nothing else to say.'

He put a hand on the door. He said 'Have you told Richard?'

'Told him what?'

'Where is he?'

'In the garden.'

'You are a faithful sister!' Harry said.

He went downstairs through a dining-room at the back and out through french windows. There was a small paved garden. Richard was kneeling at the bottom of a plane-tree. He was making a ridge of earth with his hand. Harry said 'Hullo.' Richard said 'Oh, hullo.' He looked at Harry sideways. His socks were round his ankles. Harry moved round the back of the tree.

'The most extraordinary thing has happened,' Harry said.

'Yes I know,' Richard said. His voice was matter-of-fact.

'You know?' Harry said. 'About Jules?'

'Oh no,' Richard said. 'What about Jules?'

Harry reached the garden wall and stared at it. He said 'He went and beat up the boys you had a fight with.'

Richard blushed. He pulled some bark off the plane-tree.

'He followed them yesterday,' Harry said. 'Jules won.'

'But how did he know?' Richard said.

'Didn't he?'

'I didn't tell him,' Richard said.

Harry stood over him. Richard was gazing at the tree with his bright, freckled face. Harry said 'Anyway, it happened.'

Richard squatted on his heels. The sun shone through the leaves and spread on the ground like camouflage. Harry said 'They were all arrested.'

Richard said 'Jules was?'

'There was a knife, but it's all right now, they're out.'

'How?' Richard said. He looked up quickly.

'I went round this morning. At half past six,' Harry said.

'You got them out?'

'The police rang me, they might have done before, but I don't think Jules told them.'

'The others too?'

'Well, you wouldn't want anything more, would you?'

'Oh no, no,' Richard said.

'So that's all right.'

'But why did they let them out?' Richard said. 'I mean why did they let you get them?'

'Oh well –' Harry said. He ran a hand through his

224

hair. 'They do, you see.' He laughed. 'They made jokes – you know – about how now I was so famous they were going to hand over everyone to me. Did you see that thing in the paper?'

'Oh yes,' Richard said.

'That's how it works,' Harry said. 'They like me really.' He stared at the back of the house. 'It's odd, but they do.'

Lydia appeared at a window. She called 'There was a message from Helen Mason, supposed to be important, about a man called Bill.'

'Oh no!' Harry said.

'He came to pay you back five shillings, though why that's important I can't think.'

'But it is!' Harry said.

'You can't be that hard up.'

'A revolution!' Harry said.

A telephone began ranging inside the house. Lydia said 'Oh God, what a morning!' and disappeared.

Harry said 'This is extraordinary.' He began walking round the tree.

'What?' Richard said.

Harry screwed his face up. He said 'You know Jules wanted to go to Australia?'

'Yes.'

'Well he's going.' Harry stopped, staring vertically down.

'Why's it extraordinary?'

'He made up his mind,' Harry said. 'Everything happened. The police, you, the boys, me, Father Patterson, his grandfather, Aunt Lydia – and he's going to Australia.'

The sun moved through the tree. The bark had black and silver patches on it. Lydia's voice could be heard talking on the telephone.

'It works,' Harry said. 'You don't know how, but it does. Most of the time everything's in a muddle. Then it's like a light coming on.'

'What?' Richard said.

'You haven't done it,' Harry said, 'but it happens because you've stuck at it.'

Lydia reappeared at the window. She said 'That was Annie, she sent you her love.'

'What was she on about?'

'Jerril's cut himself on his glass, you wouldn't believe it, she's taking him to the seaside.'

'Well I don't know what that means,' Harry said.

'She looks after him,' Lydia said. 'She's a saint!'

Lydia stayed at the second-floor window looking down. Harry gazed at the sky. Richard said 'How do you stick at it?'

'What?' Harry said. 'Oh you learn. Be brave.' He squatted down by Richard so that their heads were almost touching. 'Pray.' He put a hand to the tree to stop himself overbalancing. Then he said – 'Those boys will have to lump it!'

Lydia shouted from the second-floor window. 'Have you heard a word I've been saying?'

'No,' Harry said.

'I said, what time shall we start this afternoon?'

'Any time,' Harry said.

'Where are you going?' Richard said.

'Not me, you,' Harry said. 'You're going with Aunt Lydia to the country.'

'You haven't even told him?' Lydia said.

'What are you doing?' Richard said.

'What on earth have you been talking about?' Lydia said.

'I'm going to America,' Harry said.

'Are you going to see Mummy?'

'Yes, I'm going to bring her back.'

'Oh jolly good,' Richard said. He blushed.

Lydia said 'We'll start after lunch then.'

'Mummy won't be in this bomb thing in America, will she?' Richard said.

'Oh no,' Harry said. He looked at the bark of the tree. There was a black patch peeling off it. 'No, I don't think so.'

'Don't you know?' Richard said.

Harry opened his mouth; then leaned his head against the tree. There was a pain at his heart. He thought – I am too far away: there is still half a world to cross.

5

On either side of him a dividing line ran into the distance – on his left a beach with waves and white foam and on the right a high fence of wire. He was in the angle where they approached before reflecting away again behind him. In front were rough grasses and flowers growing in sand. There was no rock: only the sea and dryness where the wind blew.

Along the fence now out of sight was an entrance-and an exit-gate, with a sentry house and red-and-white striped barriers across each road. He had stepped out of his car (the heat, with the noise of crickets, had muffled him) on to the gravelled road where tar glistened. He had gone to the two armed sentries and had said (he was remembering this: he still did not find it easy to say the names) 'I have a letter from General—; I am looking for my—.' The sentry had turned into the gatehouse and had picked up a receiver and had held it under his chin. Harry had watched him through plate glass and the man had stared through a further window at the yellow sand.

Harry thought – I have been here before. The heat made the ground liquid. He had sat with a receiver under his chin and had watched the lighted windows of a huge office building opposite. There were thousands of young men now in khaki uniforms and spherical helmets and watchful, indifferent faces. They were like wirelesses with the knobs turned off. They stood at the gates of high wire fences where everything was hidden behind flat concrete buildings.

On the other side the waves came in and broke and spread on the golden sand. They were like towers falling, sucked into the crash of the incoming wave and rearing in the same leap. The sand whirled. Each grain was a crystal with perfect colours.

The fence was bent inwards at the top with four barbed strands at an angle. Below, the wire was in a criss-crossed mesh. The concrete buildings had been visible from the gate. There was a flagpole with no flag on it. He had said 'The General is my father-in-law.' The sentry had looked at him once while he telephoned and then had said 'Will you wait in your car please.' 'What's happening?' Harry had said. 'Will you wait in your car please.' The sentry was chewing. He tilted his chin into the distance as if summoning it.

The General was an old, thin man in a chair, with a smile like a skeleton. His room had had firearms on the walls. He had said 'I don't know if I can help you.' There had been dark panels and leather chairs and the bright colours of magazines. A drawing-room with embroidered covers was never used. 'I can give you a letter,' the General had said. 'How long has she been gone?' 'A few weeks,' the General had said.

The waves came in and broke and spread sideways. Harry lay on his side on the beach. The grains of sand were numberless. Each grain was a world, with crystals whirling. The towers crashed and collected themselves. Space was void.

The first time he had ever seen Melissa she had been in a crowded room against a background of wall-lamps and mirrors. Her face had appeared over the shoulder of the man she was dancing with. Harry had seen himself reflected in her. There had been a taste of salt; a roughness on the tongue like sand. Reaching down, she had been like a child.

'You must be tired,' the General had said. 'Why don't you rest up a while?'

The first time he had spoken to her (her face appearing like the moon) he had said 'Love is trusting a person as on a mountain with a rope.' 'Do you climb?' Melissa had said. 'Or in a car, with someone who does not drive.' 'I don't drive,' Melissa had said. The sky had rushed past her. They went out into the street with buildings like falling pinnacles. They sat in the car. He heard himself like a spy in a further room: 'This is the switch, this the starter.' She had a black band around her head and ears like carefully-painted flowers. 'When the engine is running you put in the clutch.' He had one arm behind her and the other along the door. They started. They rode on the back of the world, heaving. They were in the dark. When they came to a crossroads the lights came against them like bullets. Going fast, she began to scream.

'You've been flying all night,' the General had said.

He had crossed the Atlantic in a jet with a tunnel inside it like an Egyptian tomb. There were three rows

230

of figures down each side, their faces superimposed. The colours were well preserved. They were protected from the air that rots – the rays and the bright clouds.

America had not changed. Cars ran on wide rails and went over and under between pillars. Down passages of concrete the wind blew. Tall towers went into the air and stopped there. The earth was buildings and mud.

He and Melissa had never questioned marrying. Around and above them were the rock, the desert. Moving, they had shifted patterns in the sand. He had said 'When will you tell your parents?' She had said 'Now.' The wind piled the sand-dunes with fire. They were cut off from the sea and land.

There had been a church with thick round pillars and ladies in furs and beads. The organist had watched them through a mirror. Harry had seen himself standing at the top of the aisle (there were other spies now, in the gallery like cinema projectionists) and Melissa floating on veils and lilies. The General was beside her with his arm bent. Harry and she were like soldiers on a mountain pass, signalling about enemy in the valley. He held his rifle horizontal and moved it up and down. She stopped. The enemy came closer – the ladies in furs and their necks stretched with rope. He held the ring a few inches from her finger. There was music, and a man in a white robe. The enemy were with horses.

He had said to the General 'I must get on.'

The sand was transparent like amber. There was no scent. Yellow cupped flowers had leaves as thick as tongues. With your ear to the ground, the earth boomed.

After they had been married they had gone to a hot

231

shuttered room where they could hear the sea. Marriage was like a magnet; you were the two ends of a U. They had held each other; around them the world was grouped. They had lain on wooden floor-boards and the dust had arranged itself. Nets hung from the ceiling. The body was weight, knees and elbows – the elements of earth and air.

He had borrowed the General's car to come here. The houses in the suburbs were at different angles in identical plots. They had been shaken like dice. The car had one pedal, clicking over smooth rails. He had thought – what am I doing?

The flat buildings behind the wire were a hospital. There were a tall chimney and a water-tower out of sight. A ladder went up beside the tower, which was on four legs with a round top. No smoke came out of the chimney.

Bones rotted. Like leaves and branches, they went back to earth. The living had to be protected from the dying: the dying make way for unborn children. To propitiate the dying, a temple had been built in the desert.

Lying on the boards of the hot room on their honeymoon he had opened one eye and seen the dust in ridges and a white skin. Tribes in Africa put on the masks of animals. He and Melissa were naked. The wind trod over him. He was a Gulliver in sand-dunes. He was tied at his legs and fingers.

He had expected he would find Melissa again in some pose as he remembered her – against a background of wall-lamps and mirrors and with a small crowd around her. She would be in profile, one foot directly in front of the other and her two arms superimposed. Her hair was golden. There was a black band on top of it. When she laughed, her neck wrinkled. There would be three men around her – one short with thin hair and a fine nose, one dark with a heavy mouth, and one so tall that his head was out of sight. She wore her red dress. The enemy were calling.

The hospital had once been an aerodrome. Jets took off from the flat land and it became a tongue with the waves peeling. The bones went white. From a height, there were patches where the clouds fell.

Melissa had always seen the world like a hospital. Children starved and beggars lay in heaps. Her face grew hard with something archaic about the mouth. He had put out a hand and touched her. A sculptor would have changed it. When their child was born, she had softened among the flowers and trees like light.

The General had sat in his room with the dark panels and ships made of cotton and balsa wood. He had said 'They know what they're doing. What else would you want?'

A bomb like a ship's boiler was pushed out on to a runway. There were flat concrete buildings behind barbed wire. The bomb was on dozens of wheels like castors. The back of the bomb began to swing round faster than the front. It grew to a torpedo a hundred yards long and hundreds of men were chasing it. They were dressed in black, some with top hats. The front came towards them again and they turned and fled.

He had said to the sentry 'Can I wait on the beach?'

233

A wind blew along the sand-dunes. Harry lay on his side and he drew his knees up so his body would be protected. He opened one eye and saw the patch of sand close like the floor of a tent. At the far side was the mountain formed by his legs and knees. A path went over it, down which travellers never came. In the valley was a city.

Richard had been born in a hospital. There had been a small irregular room with cream walls and iron pipes. The nurse had stood at one side of the bed and the doctor at the other. Harry faced the foot, with his back against a wall. They lifted up Melissa's legs. There was a handle at the foot of the bed like a rack. The child's head had come out and stayed there. There was rubber, and the clink of knives.

Over the huge country the clouds hung like puffs. Animals moved slowly, stalking water. Water was separate from the earth, which was dry.

Melissa was beautiful. There was a picture by Fra Filippo Lippi of the Madonna in a garden with the trees coming down in green and gold. She wore a blue dress. The child was lying on the ground amongst three-petalled, carefully painted flowers. Richard had lain on the end of the bed and no one had paid attention to him. He had come out like something gutted. Afterwards he did not breathe. Harry had leaned forward, praying.

There had been a photograph in the paper of an absolutely flat landscape, blurred. A sentry stood in the foreground in his nut-shaped helmet and with a rifle. Around him were fallen walls and rubble. If you put a magnifying glass over the photograph, there would be just black dots in rows. Through a microscope one dot would take up the whole of the picture. It would be an absolutely flat landscape, blurred.

Above the child in the garden was a bird with a shaft of light. The light was a tree, growing downwards. The angels watched with their quiet, adoring faces. Richard had taken his first breath which was a sigh. They had picked him up by the heels and hit him.

From the sand in front of Harry's eyes one stem of grass grew which was yellow at the bottom and rose to a green point. The sky arched above it. The sky was a body, touching the earth at its hands and heels. The air bred monsters. They swam down with horns and wings and laid eggs in the bones that rotted.

Once he and Melissa had been staying at an enormous country house. There were wicker chairs in the bathroom and pigeons that cooed. Melissa's face was like a rock. He had put out a hand and touched her. The rock had slipped. She had fallen, clawing. She had run for the window.

Once, on their honeymoon, on the beach with the silver sand and the waves like towers, she had faced him and put her arms round his neck. She had lifted her legs and wrapped them behind him. Like this they had gone into the sea.

He had caught her by the window. Fighting, she had scratched at his face and hands. He had thought – I know how to love and to pray. In the morning, they had heard a man in the next room. Melissa had said 'He will think us passionate.'

235

'I couldn't stop her,' the General had said. 'Melissa has always – '

Harry was thirsty. There was water in the car where he had parked it. He had not eaten nor slept. He imagined himself kneeling in a desert of sand-dunes. Riders came behind him and struck at the back of his head. He went down between their hooves and cried for water. The lower part of his body was already in the earth, like leaves and branches.

Once he had gone to an upper room and locked the door and had stared into a corner with his bright clown's face. His gun had rust inside the barrel. This blew the end off. You put the gun in your mouth and reached for the trigger. Or you did it with your toe, like a sunbather.

In the heat the crowds ran towards the river. Their shadows stayed where they were. They lifted their arms up and sank without disappearing.

He held the ring a few inches from her finger. Slipping it on, the finger had become thick and bent. He held the top of it; the ring on the inside. His gun was engraved with tassels and embroidery. Looking down, he imagined they were handcuffed. The spies had sent their messages. There were men in caps with blood-hounds.

He stood with Melissa in the room with wicker chairs. He had said 'We are the same person: if we tear each other's heart out, we die.'

They had knelt in a ditch, panting. The dogs had gone past them. In a trickle of water he had seen his face. It expanded and contracted on the ripples. He bent close. The water rose up past his eyes and mind.

Running, they reached the corner of a wood. There were flat fields beyond them and a water-tower in the distance. Looking above the level of the grass, the earth curved. The enemy were in the village.

He had said to the General 'But what is happening?' 'The area is sealed off,' the General had said. (There was the sound of soldiers trotting.) 'How many were injured?' 'They are being looked after,' the General had said. (The soldiers went into the distance like cavalry at Waterloo.)

They reached a building with a few walls standing and a piece of roof. (He was imagining this.) There was a blanket hanging instead of a door. Inside was a smell of tea. Men round a table looked up. They wore steel helmets and battledress. A man said 'We've got a job for you': he smiled; his front teeth were filed to points. On the table was a paraffin lamp and a tin of fifty cigarettes.

'Melissa was trained as a nurse,' the General had said. The crowds on the beaches held their arms up, screaming.

The man at the table made room for them. They looked at a map-case covered with talc and lines in coloured pencil. There were circles and figures, and contours like a skin. A man put a thumb at the centre. There was gunfire outside.

'They wanted everyone they could get,' the General had said.

The enemy came baying through the wood like wolves. Harry was above a parapet looking through low branches. Melissa was with him. A man was shot, falling against a tree. The bark of the tree was black and dusty. The bullets came like rain. Harry began to move, going down towards the valley. Melissa stayed.

'Melissa has always – ' the General had said.

On his own, he found himself in a glade of pale trees. He put his rifle down. There was a bird like a flute playing. He walked from side to side. The bird was trying to tell him something. Melissa had been captured. There was a flower like a red iris.

He touched the flower. It was sticky, with a wrapping like paper. He picked it. It had no smell. He licked his tongue on top of his mouth.

Melissa had not been fighting. She had stood with her arms on the parapet. The General had said 'She has always wanted to help the world.'

Once at night, he had woken to find a pain in his body as if its shape were altering. He stretched but found nothing to press against. There was a rope round his neck being pulled. He kicked in the dark.

There was something he was trying to remember. He and Melissa had been on the mountain with the enemy in the valley. There was no enemy. They had run behind sand-dunes like children.

They had never questioned marrying. He had said 'When will you tell your parents?' She had said 'Now.' There had been a room like a recruiting station. The man with pointed teeth sat behind a table. He had a map-easel. He put a thumb in the middle. They had filled in a form, and were enrolled.

They walked beneath oak trees in a park where pigeons cooed. They held each other by the hand. A gun boomed. A man spoke on the wireless. It was eleven o'clock. In the church, the people stood to attention.

He had opened an eye on the floor of the shuttered room and seen the boards with cracks in them. A shell had landed. He spat the earth from his eyes, his tongue. His body was protecting hers: the wind stepped over him. They had lain in the ditch with the ring round their wrists joining them. He could see the village above the level of grass. Her eyes were open. She looked away from him, towards the sea.

He seemed to be dreaming. There was a cave, with a path going up the face of a cliff diagonally. At the front was a ledge with the remains of a fire. The tops of the trees grew to a level with the cave. The roof at the entrance was blackened.

Opposite it was a plain of white ground rising towards a mountain. At the foot was a man in a white robe. He faced a crowd, which was seated. There was no shade; the sky was a dome. The man in the robe was speaking.

Harry was on the outside, watching. There was a statue above the cave and smoke from candles. The crowd was waiting.

People had bones deformed. A boy with a huge head sat on a board on wheels. His legs were like spilled matches. He spun and came to rest, looking upwards.

The sky was in darkness. Stars fell, without moving nearer or farther away. People swarmed towards the river. An emperor walked through an empty palace. Soldiers held babies by the feet and hit them. Horsemen rode in the desert.

On the horizon a city burned. A woman rose and

239

picked up her child. She wrapped a cloak round it and kept in the shadows. On the edge of the city was a field of maize. The stalks were broken. She sat down and nursed her baby. The baby cried.

The body of the sky began to move as if its shape were altering. A ship groaned; a sail stretched in the wind. A sphere was being formed of the blue dome.

He was with Melissa on the silver beach by the sea. She put her arms round his neck and wrapped her legs behind him. He walked into the water. It was cold. She clung to him. He turned facing the land and pushed backwards so that he floated. Melissa raised herself. His body buckled, going under. They broke apart.

The pain began returning again. Opening his mouth, and feeling with his tongue where there was no moisture (only the black bark of the tree; the floorboards with the dust in them) he took his gun and put the barrels pointing towards his brain. The cold tingled like a battery. As he breathed, the pain lessened. The gun was a pipe running into the earth from his eyes and brain. There was a plunger in it, drawing his inside upwards. He groped for it. The trigger-guard bulged like a petal.

Sitting on the wooden floor of the shuttered room he had looked for an escape. There was a slope going down from the trench past the branches. It led to the valley and the glade. Melissa's wrist was still tied to his, hanging limply. She had soft hands. He looked up to her shoulder which was white like a tree stripped of bark. An axe whirled. He jumped, feeling the metal against his mouth.

The officers sat round the table in the dug-out. The

man with pointed teeth smiled. A body was brought in upon a stretcher.

He was in a dry hollow of grass and sand. (He remembered the glade; or remembered there was something he might remember.) He had walked across a desert from a temple with tall gold pillars and capitals like palm-trees. In the hollow there was no wind; only the buzz of insects. Sweat ran down his fingers. There were stone statues lying on their backs. They had goats' heads and the bodies of women. Dragon-flies flew round with bodies joined by a thread. There was a pond beyond with green water.

In the night another sun appeared. It gave no light to anything around it, but was visible itself like a torch shone into the eyes. Harry put out the palm of his hand. At the top of his mind a figure began to run away, climbing out of the trench past the line of blackened branches. Melissa made a noise like an animal. The wood bayed. He was a mind; a million particles. One arm was holding up the sky.

The bright light grew. The crowd began moving towards the mountains. They passed the entrance to the cave where the ceiling was blackened. The boy on wheels went with them.

In the valley was the city of thick stone pillars. Birds flew into holes beneath the capitals. There was a chattering of starlings and the smell of bats. Writing was round the walls in high letters. A narrow staircase led towards the roof.

He saw water coming in beneath a door. It formed a pool and swelled round the legs of chairs and tables.

There had been a spring uncovered; someone had kneeled and scratched. The stream was spreading round the earth.

The crowd on the mountain waited. The light flickered in their faces. The woman uncovered the face of her child and offered it her breast. On its cheek she saw a faint mark, which crumbled. She looked and saw the faces of the crowd half-goat, half-human. The water was rising.

In the city a crowd moved past the doors of empty houses. A tower began to fall. It broke like a wave and reared again in dust. In the dug-out the man closed his map-case with two metal studs. He said 'Gentlemen!' Outside was the sound of machine-guns. They went out through the blanket over the door and stood by the fields in front of the village. The village was burning with the water-tower silhouetted against flames. A searchlight reflected on the bases of clouds. Tracers from machine-guns floated in the air like fireflies.

At the top of the staircase was a small open courtyard. There were two statues. One was of a half-boy, half-woman, with the face curving convexly to the end of nose and lips. The other had a goat's head and two pointed teeth. They were each stepping forward, their feet exactly parallel, their arms straight by their sides.

The pain within him grew intense. People stood with only their top halves visible. Within his legs he felt numbness like water rising. He tried to let the pain float away, and it came back like a stick on the waves. The night was teeming. Bodies were pressed close. They moved like scum.

The woman with the child turned her back and saw the clouds going past her. She covered the child's head. The space around her rushed outwards. She placed the child on the ground and lay around it, her body forming a circle to protect it. She put her cloak over the two of them, so that the inside was like a tent. The air grew warmer.

The people round the table had gone. The water rose to the heads of the statues. The spray was coming along the top of the waves like the sun.

He saw Melissa with her fair head and the black band round it and her beautiful slightly convex face with its curves of nose and mouth. She was with the crowd moving towards the sea. He tried to approach her but he found that he could not run. He sprang high in slow motion at each step and was blown back by the wind. He shouted for her. Then he let himself go, curving his body with his head down by his knees. The wind took him. It blew him round and he swung close to the earth then rose slightly and was being carried along a few feet off the ground and parallel to it. He saw himself approaching a barbed wire fence and the concrete legs of the water-tower. He straightened himself.

Inside the hollow the baby opened its mouth and took a breath like a sigh. The body of the woman was a rock. The baby stretched its arms to the covering above it. It touched the blue and violet sky.

In front of him Harry could see the whole curve of the earth. The water spread in long white lines and at their convergence a bubble formed as if something were being born there. Harry held it in his hands. Then the wind that was carrying him changed direction and blew straight upwards, taking him with it. He rocketed. He felt the pain inside him dropping away with the air and the speed; and he was high and floating at the base of violet clouds. He held out his arms, swimming. The clouds were superimposed on one another with their edges moving. They drew apart and he saw through them a blue and silver light of shapes and angles. Each shape (which was tiny) was set in a different plane, which made them infinite. He turned, keeping himself watching. Then he began to fall towards the earth; awakening.

Harry felt the sand dead and tasteless against his mouth. His body had grown stiff with his head bent down towards his knees. He stretched and lay on his back and opened one eye and shielded it and saw the glare at first white and then changing to blue beyond his hand. There was the barbed wire fence on one side of him, and on the other the long lines of the sea.

On the beach was a solitary figure. The yellow and green grass blew on the sand-dunes. There were two dunes between him and the sea. Harry knelt up. There were lumps of black tar and leaves like thistles. A piece of wood had white lines on it.

Harry began walking at right angles to the beach round the nearest dune. Coming round the side, he saw the beach empty. The dunes made smooth curves to a hollow. As he walked the edges became superimposed again.

The fence on the other side was of criss-crossed wire

to a height of eight feet. Stakes were ten yards apart and silver-painted. They had holes in them to which the wire was fastened by links.

Round the edge of the second dune he saw the sea again and Melissa standing by it. She wore a red-and-grey skirt and a white blouse. Her hair was shorter than he remembered. She had seen him and was facing along the waves. He was approaching round the hollow of the second dune. The sand was thick and he slid back at each step. Melissa moved towards him. She walked with her feet directly forwards and her arms by her sides. There was a small ridge between them. The sand was wrinkled. He lifted a foot high. Melissa wore brown shoes with the ends of the laces hidden. She had no stockings. There was a scar on one leg where she had once been torn on barbed wire. A belt like a girth was at her waist. He took her by the arms and leaned towards her and she touched him with her cheek. Her face was soft. The waves behind her were in tiers.

They came in sight of the gate walking hand in hand. On the road was the car that he had borrowed from her father. The two sentries stood by the gate. They had steel helmets and rifles.

Through the gate with its red-and-white barriers was a guardroom with a window with a ledge outside it. A jeep stood beyond. A sergeant leaned out of the window, chewing. Melissa spoke to him in her carefully enunciated voice. 'Can – Mr Gates – come in – please?' The sergeant brushed at his sleeve as if an insect had landed on it: 'He's – all – yours – ma'am.' 'I think – we'll walk,' Melissa said. The sergeant swivelled his head and screwed up his eyes into the sun. He said 'There are snakes – in them – hills.' Melissa lowered her eyes. They went through the gates, still holding hands. Melissa said 'He is cheeky.'

She put her head against Harry's shoulder. The road ran over the dunes so that each horizon was close. The heat made the road shimmer. There were bumps like bubbles. In the distance was the water-tower on its four concrete legs. A ladder ran beside it.

The air was dry and made his throat contract. There were scattered flints and pieces of concrete with iron. 'Is Richard all right?' Melissa said. 'Yes, he's all right,' Harry said.

They came over the brow of a hill and saw the low concrete buildings in front of them. Each building had a path round it with a border of sand like a flowerbed. The paths were marked with white stones. The buildings were joined by black-roofed wooden passages, into which there were doors without handles like exits to a cinema. The windows in the buildings were hinged at the top and propped open at the bottom with sticks.

Melissa pushed on a door. The walls inside the passage were in slats overlapping horizontally. The window-frames were of unpainted wood with rusty fastenings. The floor was concrete. At the end there were double doors with glass in the top halves and beyond them a long room with hospital beds. The beds had black-painted iron ends and grey blankets. People lay with their arms by their sides and their heads turned horizontally.

A nurse came through the double doors carrying an

246

object under a cloth. As she passed Henry saw where the cloth had dipped down and become wet. The nurse had grey hair and spectacles.

Melissa turned through another door with EXIT on it in green letters and they were out in the sun again in a three-sided square with paths and flower-beds of sand. Through the triangles of horizontally-raised shutters he could see the hospital ward with beds again. There was a man in pyjamas with his head bandaged. His eyes were open. From the open end of the square Harry saw more concrete buildings stretching away in rows. Beyond them was a bulldozer crawling on a grey hill. There was a chimney like a factory, with no smoke. The road appeared again and went over a near horizon. A basketball goal-post leaned at an angle.

They went up a path bordered with white stones to a wooden hut with black roofing and yellow-painted windows. There were doors along it, each with a metal number. Melissa took from her skirt a bunch of keys on an iron ring. Her hair had parted at the neck so that strands hung down in front of her shoulders. Her shoes were worn on the inside at the heels. She unlocked the door and there was a small room with a bed and a table and a wardrobe and a wash-stand with a bucket. On the bed was Melissa's brown suitcase with clothes and newspaper in it. A leather strap stuck up. Her flowered sponge-bag was on the wash-stand.

Harry sat on the bed. There was a photograph of Richard and underneath it some letters. The frame of the photograph was of silver. Richard was about six years old, in profile. Through the open window on the far side of the room Henry saw the bulldozer shaking on the grey mound. It changed gear, its tracks going round without its moving. Melissa had opened the door of the wardrobe, which was empty. Her suitcase had an old label on it saying *Southampton Central*. 'How long have you been here?' Harry said. 'About a fortnight,' Melissa said. The bulldozer shook and pushed earth over the brow of the hill. Harry picked up one of the letters which was in Richard's neat, copperplate hand. *Dear Mummy, this is the last week of term.* Underneath was a telephone message written in pencil. *General Adams will ring again this evening.*

Melissa had finished packing and she closed the lid of her suitcase. There were zip-fasteners round each side. They each took one and pulled and fastened them into a clip in the middle. 'I'll take it to the car,' Harry said. Some men went past the window pushing a trolley. Harry remembered somewhere a factory chimney with smoke; a smell of scorching and shelters like bathhouses. Melissa sat on the bed.

The sun made narrow shadows from the walls of the concrete buildings. There were drainpipes going down from the flat roofs. Melissa began to cry. She made a gentle noise with her head down and her hands on the edge of the bed. He put his hand on hers. 'You're all right, you can go?' he said. Tears ran down her face on to the red-and-grey skirt. It had a pocket which was fastened with a concave bone button. 'Yes,' Melissa said. There was a smell of fertilizer as if from dusty fields. The wind blew it. He put his arm round her shoulders and held her. He said 'It's all right, we had to get away.'

'I know.' Melissa said. 'Both of us, for a bit,' Harry said. She put her head on his shoulder. 'It's just been so awful,' she said.

He picked up her suitcase. She followed him out of the door and they stood in the sun on the sand with the white stones in paths along it. She had brushed her hair so that it hung smoothly down her neck. She said 'I must leave the keys.' She went down the path and through a green swing door. He looked at his clothes. He was wearing dark grey trousers and brown shoes with rubber soles. He had undone his collar when he had been waiting by the beach. His shirt had a check pattern and had come apart at the waist. His hands were marked with tar.

Melissa came out of the swing doors and waited for him on the road. She set off slightly ahead of him with her fair hair bouncing. There was a tendon like a tree down her long neck to her collar-bone. Around her eyes were pale faintly luminous patches of silver. The flesh around her ears was soft, and the edges of her mouth. Her face was golden. She held a coat and a handbag in one arm while the other swung to and fro. Her feet pointed directly in front of her. She waited for Harry to come up and took his arm. 'How are we going home?' she said. 'By air,' Harry said.